A Captain Hook, Crocodile,
& Wendy Darling Reimagining

DEVOUR THE DARK

NIKKI ST. CROWE

NIKKI ST CROWE

CONTENT WARNINGS
FOR THE DEVOURER SERIES

Graphic language, violence, abusive parent, verbally abusive parent/parent who uses derogatory language towards child, internal struggles with sexual identity/internal struggle of self due to parental abuse, graphic sexual content, mentions of spousal coma/death, blood drinking, captive/captivity, submission, talk of suicide, war, death of family

For a more comprehensive list of all of Nikki's work, please visit her website below.

https://www.nikkistcrowe.com/content-warnings

ACKNOWLEDGMENTS

This series would not be possible without the help of several people.

First and foremost, thank you to Jeff for sensitivity reading Devourer of Men and the relationship between James Hook and the Crocodile.

A huge thank you to Kylie @kylies.booknook for sensitivity reading for Asha.

I will be forever grateful for helping me to accurately and respectfully portray these characters. Any mistakes or inaccuracies that remain in this series are entirely my own.

I also want to thank you, the reader, for showing up for the Lost Boys and James, Roc, and Wendy. I love these characters and this world and I count myself lucky to be writing their stories.

And lastly, thank you to JV St. Crowe, my number one hype man and best friend. I appreciate all of the plot chats, character discussions, and endless support. If I was in a Why Choose Romance, you'd be my favorite husband.

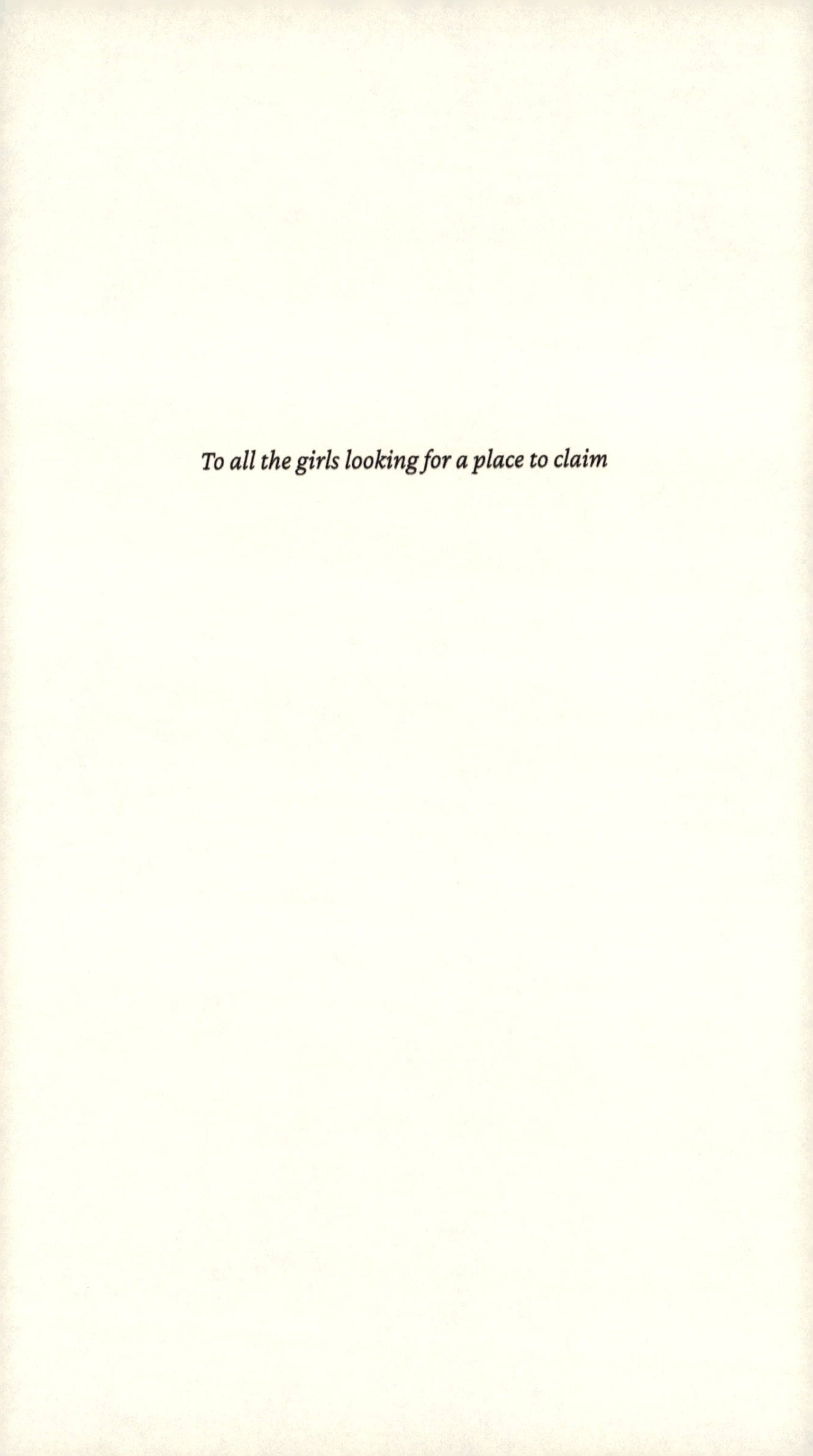

To all the girls looking for a place to claim

PROLOGUE
ROC

He had a name once and a family.

He can hear his father telling him all of the ways he has disappointed both.

He can feel the chill of the mercury against his skin, quickly followed by the burn. Being a monster, he was impossible to discipline. There were only two things that could touch him. His father thought the blade was too barbaric, but a mercury burn? It wasn't much different than a slap, was it?

You are the bane of my existence.

Sometimes, when he is alone with his thoughts, his name will burble up from memory, almost like a ghost. Fitting because that part of him is dead.

He is restless in his bed.

Everything hurts.

It would be better if he *were* dead.

He does not get sick.

He's immortal and invincible.

Pain is supposed to be fleeting.

But this is different, and that's how he knows something is wrong.

As his form shifts back and forth, too much, too often, he is pulled from the present into the past and back again until he's not sure which part of him is real.

There are the shadows of the Hall of Bones.

The silence of Maddred Manor.

The smoke of the Umbrage.

The taste of rum and tobacco on his tongue.

There is the desperation of losing all of the things he loves.

There is the chilling terror of being alone.

Then the anger that turned into apathy until he loved nothing and no one. Until he was responsible for nothing. Until his heart went from beating red to darkest black.

He has no regrets, he tells everyone, but he is full of lies.

His nearest regret is sitting in the chair beside his bed...

...begging him to be okay.

CHAPTER ONE
HOOK

I HAVE DEMANDED SILENCE FROM EVERYONE, DEMANDED CHERRY hide below decks, out of sight. There is only the sound of the waves carrying us across the sea and the creaking of the ship as it navigates the choppy waters.

The Crocodile is sleeping restlessly. Mist is lifting from him like a blackened wick, the flame snuffed out. He can't hold himself together. It's been days since we left Everland and he has not shown any improvement.

My panic has grown with each passing day.

You will be okay, I've told him. Over and over again, as if the more I say it, the truer it will become. As if he's ever followed any of my orders or listened to any of my advice.

Please be okay, I think instead. *I am begging you.*

The Crocodile tangles in the sheets, his eyes flickering back and forth beneath his closed lids.

Did I speak aloud?

I sit as still as I can in the wingback chair in the corner of my room at the back of my ship.

Don't move, you idiot. Don't breathe. Don't say a word. Poor form.

In the days since we left Everland, there is no telling what will set him off. He is an unpredictable monster with very sharp teeth and a void inside of him that never seems to be filled.

What is he? How do I stop him?

This has plagued me since the first time I saw him shift.

When he's in his monstrous form, he is no man. He's all shadow and mist, with two hollows for eyes and a bottomless maw.

I've never seen anything like him in the Seven Isles. Smee knew he needed blood to stave off his transformation, but that seemed to be where her knowledge ended.

What are you?

He shifts again, and his arm turns to pure shadow before reforming.

He has a Myth Maker witch stuck inside of him.

Did he not know the consequences of devouring her? How could he be so reckless?

I inhale, trying to quell the rapid thumping of my heart. The Crocodile has heightened senses, likely even in sleep, and I don't want my panic to wake him.

Please be okay. I am begging you.

I glance at the circular window on the starboard side of the ship searching the horizon line. Still daylight, enough to see by, but the glass of the window has grown murky with sea salt.

How much longer until we reach Neverland? I'm anxious to get answers but apprehensive about returning to the island. When Peter Pan forbade me from its shores, did that include water and port? If he spots my ship approaching, will he fly out to meet us and sink us on sight?

Christ. This is an impossible situation. But I have to risk it. There is no other choice.

The Crocodile settles back into a quiet sleep, his arm tucked beneath the pillow. Dark veins twist and branch off beneath his pale flesh, several of them thick and swollen in his forearm.

He's naked—his last meal left his clothing torn and bloody—and the sheet skims his body like water. The fabric is tucked around his waist and tangled around his legs, leaving one thigh out and the other beneath. There are more tattoos on his left thigh, ones I've yet to study. When we've been unclothed, we are, *generally speaking, preoccupied.*

I take a tentative step closer. Hold my breath as I do.

The ink is black and grey, and it depicts a cemetery with an ivy-covered gate with a name twisted into the metal. MADDRED, it reads. Several tombstones are poking up from the earth. Most of them are far in the background, impossible to read, but there are three in front.

Vane. Lane. And—

The bedroom door creaks open and my gaze jerks away from the Crocodile's body to Wendy taking up the space in the doorway. The delicate skin beneath her eyes is puffy and dark. Neither she nor I have been sleeping. We've been surviving on coffee and brandy. The brandy helps the nerves. The coffee helps keep us awake.

When the Crocodile transforms and goes after my crew, it's Wendy and me who pull him out. He won't respond to anyone else, so we always have to be ready and on high alert.

"We've spotted land," Wendy whispers, and I let out a relieved breath.

Neverland fast approaches then.

I turn away from the bed and follow her out the door, locking the Crocodile in.

Not that it would stop him.
Doors mean nothing to monsters.

CHAPTER TWO

ASHA

Wendy and Hook are arguing in hushed but heated voices.

Ever since Hook discovered the Crocodile devouring one of his men, we've been whispering.

We're all afraid of waking the Crocodile.

But Hook's men, they're whispering about a mutiny. They want to throw the Crocodile overboard.

I think Hook would consider tossing his *men* overboard if he didn't need them to feed the Crocodile.

"Peter Pan was very clear about it," Hook is telling Wendy. "I'm not allowed on Neverland soil."

"Fuck Peter Pan," Wendy says, her hands on her hips. I've seen her like this many times before. Determined, a little stubborn, maybe a little blinded by her desperation.

I've also heard that name a hundred times.

Sometimes she would mutter it like a curse, other times she would utter it like a cry.

Peter Pan. Peter Pan.

I can't tell if we should be more afraid of the Crocodile or Pan. Maybe they are equally dangerous.

"You are out of your mind!" Hook huffs out a sigh and

turns away. He bows his head. Beyond him, through the windows of the starboard dining room, land is rising up on the horizon, the sun setting behind it, painting its peaks and valleys in swashes of orange.

Neverland.

Hook and the Crocodile are not allowed on Neverland soil, as decreed by Peter Pan. And Hook won't allow Wendy to go, even though she's trying hard to convince him otherwise.

He seems to have forgotten she's a queen. She seems to have forgotten, too. I'm not quite sure why she's taking his orders, but I'm not one to get in the middle of a relationship I have no business being in the middle of.

I sharpen my blade as they continue arguing.

I like to keep my mind busy, but absent intellectual pursuits, keeping my hands busy is the next best thing.

The blade scrapes against the whetstone.

I like the sound of steel against stone. It scratches a primal itch deep down in my brain.

As my mother liked to tell it, I came out of the womb with sharp edges. "They could hear my screams in every corner of the Imperial Palace." She would smile, not fond of the pain but the pride. She would quickly add, "Never let anyone dull your edges. The world will never be your blade. You must be your own."

Thinking of my mother makes my head pound and my chest ache.

I have put my past behind me, but sometimes the rage boils up, catching me off guard.

The blade scrapes harder, louder.

Hook downs a glass of something amber in color.

Neverland grows nearer.

Wendy crosses her arms over her chest. "Then tell me,

James, what do you propose we do? Roc said he needed Vane. Vane is on Neverland and—"

"I'll go."

They both turn to look at me.

"You will?" Wendy asks.

I don't like volunteering. I learned a long time ago not to bend myself to others' will.

But truth be told, I would like to see Peter Pan for myself.

My first job after escaping Winterland was on Darkland in the Dark Archives. I spent months working between all seven branches, cataloging books so old, they creaked when you opened them. My favorite subject, beyond languages, is mythology because in the Isles, there is almost always truth to them.

The chimera. The basilisk. Seven different types of fae. The banshee and the siren. The shapeshifter and the kraken.

While working in Archive Six, I'm almost positive my superior officer was a shapeshifter. Sometimes, when he came within the bloom of a fire within the hearth, his face would ripple, almost like a mirage. Fire and shapeshifters do not mix.

I always wondered if he was on the run and had taken on a new identity. Darkland has plenty of unsavory people, plenty of bad men and women a person might need to hide from.

But I digress.

Throughout all seven archives, none of the scholars, none of the experts, seemed to have an answer as to what Peter Pan is.

Some said he was an abomination.

Some said he was a dark spirit that burbled up from the Neverland lagoon.

Some said he was an abandoned child turned wild by the Neverland forest.

Any scholar or researcher knows that witnessing something with your own eyes will always supersede reading about it.

I slide my blade into the sheath at my hip. "We can't keep losing crew members to the Crocodile's appetite. Someone needs to go. I'll go. Give me directions to the tree-house." I down the last swill of my brandy. It's late in the day now, nearing dusk, the sunlight edged in pink.

"It could be dangerous," Wendy starts.

"She's in more danger if she doesn't go," Hook counters.

Wendy scowls at him.

I'm not entirely sure how their relationship might have transformed in the last few days we've been at sea, but I think the state of the Crocodile has them both on edge.

The Crocodile is another of those myths that I'm still a bit vague on.

In the Dark Archives, his name is cited seven hundred thirty-four times but only by 'Crocodile.' His birth name seems to have been expunged from the records, either by him or someone else.

The facts I know about him are:

1. He is old—older than I am—but there is no consensus on how old. He is older than Hook and Wendy but not as old as Peter Pan.

2. The Crocodile is a member of The Bone Society, one of the Isle's secret societies. The Bone Society is credited with inventing time as we know it.

3. The roster of the Bone Society is secret, though I suspect the list is short. Because members are some kind of

unknown creature that needs blood to stave off trans-forming and devouring everything in their wake. But there is no scientific name for their kind, which leads me to believe their origins are either hidden for a reason, or they aren't from this realm.

4. The Crocodile is Vane's older brother. Vane is a Lost Boy, Peter Pan's most trusted friend. The Crocodile and Vane come from a well-known, wealthy family of Darkland. The Maddred family. They are often cited together as the Madd brothers. Their father was Duke of Maddred for a time, with Roc expected to inherit the title. Until their father tried to overthrow the monarchy, and their family was stripped of all their possessions and titles. Afterward, Vane and the Crocodile worked their way up through the ranks of the darker side of Darkland known as the Umbrage.

5. The Crocodile and Vane ruled the Umbrage for over a decade.

6. There is no mention of their mother anywhere. She, too, has been expunged from the archives.

After the Umbrage, their story gets messy and a bit murky.

Someone did something they shouldn't have, and their little sister, Lane, was murdered by the royal family as punishment. That's when Vane hunted down and took on the Darkland Dark Shadow and killed the royal family.

His actions threw Darkland into civil war. But he was long gone by then, and so was the Crocodile.

Vane is fifth on my list of intriguing figures I'd love to study, just after Peter Pan, the Crocodile, and Hansel and Gretel.

So, really, going to the treehouse is to my benefit.

"Follow the main street from Darlington Harbor southeast," Hook explains. "You'll cross Mysterious River. By then you're nearly there. Stay on the same road and it'll lead you right to the house."

"How long should we give you before we come looking?" Wendy asks.

"An hour? Maybe a little more. I'm not worried." I go to her and give her a hug. Her shoulders tremble in my embrace. She's trying to keep it together. She's trying not to cry.

She has just escaped a kingdom that kept her prisoner, first in a cold cell, then in a castle.

She has left one fear for another.

I can't shoulder that fear for her, but I can help her through it.

"It's going to be okay," I tell her.

She nods against my shoulder. I hear her take in a long breath to settle the tears.

Once, when a superior officer in the Everland Guard went too hard on me in a practice yard, it was Wendy who took care of me after. She thinks she is weak, often forgetting the kind of fortitude it requires to have compassion for other people when it's so much easier to pretend they do not exist.

"Thank you, Asha," she whispers.

When I pull away from her, her eyes are glassy.

"Thank me when I've brought the Crocodile his brother."

HOOK'S DIRECTIONS ARE ACCURATE, GIVING ME A FLASH OF satisfaction.

I like facts and I like accuracy and I like rules and I like being able to depend on all three.

I'm standing in front of the treehouse within twenty minutes of leaving the ship.

All around me, the forest crowds in. Palm trees rustle in the ocean breeze. Ferns and local flora grow among the trees, dotting the landscape in a rainbow of colors.

Firecrackers and lilies and opalassos.

Neverland is considered a tropical climate. So unlike the Winterland Alps where I come from, where the air is always crisp, the water always cool.

I scan the treehouse directly in front of me.

It's impressive, the name suitable.

A giant tree grows out of the middle of a house with a wraparound porch and several stories stacked haphazardly on top of each other. Several lampposts glow at the steps, illuminating the front door with warm light.

Crickets and spring frogs chirp in the dark.

Despite its size, the house feels cozy from this vantage point. Like a hazy dream come to life.

Hook has told me who I might encounter here, if not Peter Pan or Vane.

There are the twins, the fae princes, Kas and Bash. "Less vicious than Vane or Pan," Hook said. "But no less dangerous." Then Hook glanced at Wendy before adding, "Possibly Winnie Darling. I would be careful around her."

"Why?" Wendy had asked, confusion knitting between her brows.

"Just trust me."

Now, with my curiosity burbling to the surface, I go up the front steps, cross the front porch, and rap on the door.

CHAPTER THREE

VANE

I ALWAYS THINK OF POE WHEN I'M WITH WIN.

Deep into that darkness peering...

I think of who I was before her.

...long I stood there, wondering, fearing...

And I think about who I am now that I have her.

...dreaming dreams no mortal ever dared to dream...

Sometimes, I'm afraid she'll disappear right before my eyes.

Like a mirage, waters turning to sand, trickling through my fingers.

I never dared to dream of someone like her.

Dreams are for the weak.

"Vane," she moans and writhes beneath me.

I'm buried deep inside of her, chasing the heat of her.

The soft flesh of her thighs dimples beneath the hard press of my hands.

I hold on. I hold on tighter.

Long I stood there, wondering, fearing...

"Oh god," she says.

I rock out, push in again.

Her chest is flushed, her nipples pebbled.

Her gaze is far away and then her body starts to float up off the bed.

"Eyes on me, Win," I order, and she refocuses, her weight hitting the mattress again.

She hasn't had the Neverland shadow long, and she still loses her grip on the magic.

Especially when I'm fucking her.

Her tiny hand wraps around my wrist, anchoring her to me.

"Harder," she says on a pant.

"I fuck you any harder, I'm going to break you."

"No, you won't," she says.

I drive deeper, fully sheathed in her pussy now. The bed hates this and groans loudly, the headboard banging against the wall.

The entire house knows what we're up to, but fuck them.

Fuck all of them.

She's mine right now and I'll do with her as I please.

She whimpers, her grip on me tightening. Her body is at rest, but the magic is slipping again, and darkness spins around us.

We share the Neverland Dark Shadow, but most days, it clings to her more than me. It's with me begrudgingly because of her. And I don't fight it.

Winnie Darling is the queen of this house and the dark goddess of this island.

I'm happy to relent.

Except when we're in bed.

Then I'm in charge.

I yank the magic back, and the darkness condenses into a thick cloud.

I drive forward into her, punishing her, and she moans loudly.

"Oh fuck, oh fuck."

The darkness of the shadow ropes itself around her hips, then spills forward, down the V between her thighs before riding back up to her clit.

Win hisses in pleasure.

The darkness moves like a river, constantly in motion, teasing at her center, pulling her closer and closer to the edge.

"Vane," she says. "Fill me up."

"As if you tell me what to do."

"Vane," she moans again and the magic between us throbs, and I feel her answering clench, her pussy tightening around my cock.

I don't come until she comes. That's my rule. One I will never break.

I direct the moving darkness over her clit, covering her completely. In this moment, I and the magic possess her, teasing her to the crescendo.

"Come for me, Winnie Darling. Don't disappoint me."

She moans, high and short.

And then she's tensing up beneath me, the orgasm rushing through her.

"Oh...*god.*" She turns the word into a breathy moan.

There is no art, no magic, no poetry, no glory of nature more beautiful than Winnie fucking Darling coming on my cock.

I am in awe of her.

I am consumed by her.

The magic we share expands, darkness shimmering

around the room, and I am in the dream, dreaming no dream any man ever dared to dream.

She has me.

Every part.

Heart and soul and every dark urge.

I am hers.

And she is fucking *mine*.

I drive into her, making her take every fucking inch of me just like she asked.

And then I'm spilling inside of her, filling her up, all of the pressure rushing out of me.

She watches me beneath long lashes and heavy eyes.

She smiles when a tremor runs through me.

"I love watching you come," she tells me.

"You are a glutton."

"For Lost Boy cum," she adds.

I laugh, lean into her, and kiss her. The kiss is not the same tenor of the fucking. The kiss is desperation. A religious rite. The kiss says, *I worship you, Winnie Darling.*

"I love you," she says when I pull away. "Every day, I love you more than the day before."

"You know it terrifies me when you say that." I roll over onto the bed beside her.

"Yes. But you never tell me why."

I am not human, and with the shadow, neither is Win anymore, but I've experienced heartbreak, loss...

It's the closest I've felt to being mortal.

I'm terrified of losing her. I'm terrified of never measuring up. Terrified of my past repeating.

Win slides over, resting her head against my damp chest and I wrap my arm around her, tucking her in.

I don't have to explain any of this to her. I know she knows it.

The shadow makes hiding things from each other annoyingly difficult.

"I love you too," I whisper into her hair and close my eyes and drink in the scent of her.

This moment is mine, but it won't be for much longer.

The sun is setting, which means Pan will be up, and I can hear the twins in the kitchen preparing Win a meal.

But I'll take whatever few minutes I can get.

"What should we do today?" she asks me.

I play with the ends of her hair. "Pan wants to check on the land."

Now that the fae and the Lost Boys are united, we've decided to build a new castle for all. The land is being prepared with construction beginning soon.

Win groans against me. "I want to have a bonfire and a party."

"Pan will tell you no."

"That's why you should suggest it."

I shift on the pillow so I can meet her eyes. There is a lock of hair over her forehead, so I swipe it back, and she arches toward me, always desperate for my touch.

"I would never suggest a party. He knows me better than that."

She groans again. "Maybe you and Pan can go check on the land while Kas, Bash, and I have a party."

"You think Pan will allow you to get drunk with the twins? Think again."

Pan has learned to give up some of his control over our Darling, but there are some things he will never relent on. He's too possessive to allow her to have too much fun outside of his careful eye.

He's lost too much to grow complacent. We all have.

"Okay, well then—"

She's cut off by a knocking on the front door.

We don't get many visitors these days. It used to be Lost Girls showing up on our doorstep looking for a good time, but not anymore. Not only do we have the one and only woman we will ever need, but Winnie Darling would gut them for even considering it.

I climb out of bed and pull on pants. Win is up and slipping into her dress a second later.

"Are we expecting anyone?" she asks me.

"Not that I'm aware of."

Winnie follows me down the hall into the loft where the Never Tree is glowing with pixie bugs.

Voices filter up from the foyer.

Kas and Bash are at the front door, shirtless, their wings folded against their backs.

There's a girl on the stoop. No one I recognize.

"I'm here for Vane," she tells the twins.

"Sorry," Bash says. "Vane is occupied."

"And not interested," Kas adds.

They start to shut the door, but the girl shoves her foot in, blocking it. She's quick, brave.

"It's important," she insists.

"Doubtful," Bash says. "Everything of importance is here, under our roof. So if you would kindly fuck off—"

"It's about his brother."

Win and I share a look.

Roc left the island not long after Captain Hook. Pan forbade him from returning. Apparently, my brother tried to kill Pan. Or he helped Pan figure out his true form by killing him. I'm still unclear on the details, and honestly, I don't really fucking care.

Hand trailing along the banister, I make my way down with Winnie right behind me. The shadow likes it when we stay close. I often use it as an excuse to keep her near.

When I come up behind Kas and Bash, they step aside, revealing the girl in the early evening light.

If I had to place her island, I'd say Winterlander. She has the straight black hair and deep brown eyes of the people who call the Winterland Alps home.

She takes in the sight of me in nothing but pants, starting with my feet, then up to my chest, landing finally on my face.

I'm used to people hungering for me. I know what I look like. It's annoying if I'm fucking honest. As if the only thing interesting about me is my appearance. If someone stares too long, I immediately know their measure: shallow, dull, *pathetic*.

But the girl's interest isn't hungry. It's distantly curious. Lacking that raw edge of hunger. Almost academic.

Almost like she wants to pin me to a board and study me.

That might be worse than lust.

"Whatever my brother has done," I say, "it has no bearing on me. Whatever you're here to tell me, I don't care." I turn away and expect Winnie to follow.

But she doesn't.

She takes a step down, then another. "How do you know Roc?" she asks the girl.

I pause beneath the Never Tree. The pixie bugs buzz above me as if they sense the rising tide of tension.

"I don't know him well," the girl answers. "I've only just met him."

"So then why are you here on his behalf?"

I hear the girl inhale. It's a breath of preparation, the kind that proceeds an important detail.

The showman's reveal.

I turn back.

"To be honest, I'm more so here on behalf of my best friend."

"And who is that?"

"Wendy," she says. "Wendy Darling."

CHAPTER FOUR

VANE

She's pacing the loft, the Neverland Shadow ribboning around her.

When she is excited, stressed, agitated, or angry, the shadow reacts, trailing her like a cape made of mist.

My shadow never did anything of the sort. It and I were always at odds. There was no sense of collaboration between us. I hunted it down, demanded its swift hand of revenge. It was hungry, so it complied. But everything after that—after I destroyed the Darkland royal family—was fraught with conflict.

It hated being on Neverland. Neverland was not its home.

But this dark shadow claimed Winnie as much as she claimed it.

They were made for one another. When she needs it, it's there. When it needs something from her, she immediately responds.

Sometimes I feel like the unwitting third party to their symbiotic relationship.

Not that I will complain. Winnie and the shadow saved me, and sharing it means I get to keep an eye on her in a way the others cannot.

"Wendy Darling is my great-great-great grandmother," Winnie is saying. "I want to meet her. I should have that right."

Pan is awake. The twins are here. The girl, Asha, is waiting outside on the front porch for our answer.

It seems Roc has devoured something he shouldn't have. Now he needs me to fix him.

I have my suspicions as to what he wants, but I don't have it. I can't help him.

"I was very clear," Pan says. "Hook and Roc are not allowed on my land."

"Your land?" Win turns on him.

Peter Pan is a god, but when Winnie Darling scowls at him, he is reduced to a man.

"Come on, Darling," Kas says, grabbing hold of her around the waist. His touch is gentle, a little coaxing. But I can tell he's trying to prevent her from charging at Pan.

Now that Win has the shadow, she has a claim to Neverland too. We all do. The twins, Kas and Bash, possess the Neverland Shadow of Life. We all, equally, have a claim.

But Peter Pan has been here the longest. Once Neverland's king, he sometimes likes to pull rank. Win likes to remind him that the past is no longer.

Now, she is queen to his king.

"I want to meet my ancestor." Win slips out of Kas's grip and puts her hands on her hips. "Remember Wendy Darling, Pan? The one you abandoned on Everland?"

Pan closes his eyes and summons a breath. No one on this island, not even me, could get away with half of the things Win gets away with. Pan might sometimes make her pay for her brattiness in the bedroom, but here, right now, her stubbornness will make him bend.

I already know it. He knows it. I'm not sure why he's still dragging his feet.

"Fine," he says and then scoops up a glass of whisky and slings it back. "We'll go to the docks. We'll meet Wendy. We'll see what Roc wants. But then they're gone."

Win crosses her arms over her chest. "Fine."

"Fine," Pan repeats.

They stare at one another for several beats. The tension is thick enough to braid.

When they get like this, they are either two seconds away from shouting at one another or two seconds away from fucking.

But we don't have time for that.

I step between them, diffusing the tension. "Let's get to the docks before it gets too late. Before my brother does something stupid and we all have to murder him."

Pan ticks out a breath. "How about we just murder him and forget about the rest?"

Behind us, Bash says to his brother, "This should be fun."

"No one is murdering anyone," Winnie says, charging ahead.

She may boss us around with impunity, but when it comes to the Crocodile, she will have no say.

She thinks she knows us, she thinks she has peered into the darkness and taken its measure.

But Roc and I, we are a darkness that cannot be tamed and I will do everything in my power to keep her away from it.

CHAPTER FIVE
WENDY

Asha stands beside me on the quarterdeck. Most of the crew have abandoned the ship now that we're docked. The ship is silent. The Neverland docks are bustling though. I never made it this far from the treehouse when Peter Pan kidnapped me and brought me to Neverland.

Was it always like this? Full of life and possibility and ordinariness?

Neverland had always felt like a fairytale to me, like an untamed forest with teeth. From this vantage point, the city spreads out in every direction. The buildings are not unlike the old timber and plaster buildings of Everland, but it's clear Neverland has started to expand and refashion. Amongst the timber and plaster are buildings of fresh stonework.

Smoke rises up from clay stacks, billowing against an ever-darkening sky and throughout the city streets, lamp-posts are lit with flame, the golden light flickering over the cobblestones.

Our port is directly across from a market street where,

despite the late hour, most of the shops remain open, offering food, drink, and wares.

I was dreading coming back here. It's not a place I have fond memories of—but seeing it now...

I breathe out and clasp my hands behind my back. I am no longer terrified of Neverland. I am no longer at the mercy of Peter Pan or his Lost Boys.

The sudden release of all of that pent-up anxiety makes my eyes burn.

"Talk to me," Asha says.

She returned to the ship about twenty minutes ago with the news that Pan, Vane, and Winnie Darling were on their way.

I'm buzzing with anticipation, fraught with emotion. I swallow, trying to hold the tears at bay. "I don't know what to say. Neverland was just a blink in my history, but it held a lot of power over me. Being here again, having the opportunity to meet one of my descendants...it's a lot."

Asha follows my gaze over the city streets.

Down below, on the docks, two men push handcarts stacked with crates. Hay sticks out of the slats. An orange tabby cat trails behind the last man, meowing loudly. "I ain't got no food for ya," he tells the cat, but the cat doesn't seem to buy it.

"And Peter Pan?" Asha asks.

A breath stutters down my throat and my stomach spins. Not in a good way.

All those long months in the Everland prison, and later in an Everland palace, I hated Roc and Hook for not rescuing me. But I hated Peter Pan more. Not because he'd abandoned me. But because he'd taken my home from me, swept me into the magic and mystery of Neverland, introduced me to Roc and Hook, and then quickly snatched it all away.

If it wasn't for Pan, I never would have met Roc and Hook and my heart would have never broken into a million fucking pieces.

Sometimes, when I lay in my bed in the palace, I would daydream about what my life might have looked like without Peter Pan and the Darling curse. I'm sure it would have been quiet, mundane, maybe even boring.

Would I have preferred that?

When I was desperate to escape, I told myself I did.

But now, standing here on James Hook's quarterdeck, a best friend beside me, just moments away from meeting my descendant who, in our realm, I would have never had the chance to meet, I think maybe I'm lucky.

I am who I am today because of everything that came before. How could I possibly wish for it to change now?

"Peter Pan," I repeat and let out a sigh. "If I see him today, I'm afraid I may stab him."

Asha pulls her blade from the sheath at her hip. "Might I suggest this blade?"

I glance at it, then up at her. We both laugh.

"What do you know about Pan?" I ask.

A sea breeze lifts the hair along her face. She has most of it twisted back and held in place with a hair stick. This is Asha prepared to fight. I only ever see her hair down when she's relaxed, when she feels safe.

"I fell down a Peter Pan rabbit hole one summer in the Dark Archives. I had heard stories about him as a child. They were mostly cautionary tales about the demise of his friendship with Tinkerbell. Tales about loyalty and betrayal."

Asha's voice catches on the word *betrayal* and though

she's never said much about what led to her running away from her home island, I've always known deep down it had something to do with betrayal.

"The scholars were never able to come to a consensus as to what Peter Pan is." Asha turns to me. "Do you know?"

I shake my head. "Whatever secrets he had, he wasn't about to share them with me."

"And now your descendant is here with him. How do you feel about that?"

The wind shifts again and I catch the scent of something sweet roasting in the city.

"I'm worried she doesn't know what she's gotten herself into. But, at the same time, I still feel like the girl I was when Pan took me, and if I'm still a girl, what do I know about protecting her anyway? What if I'm delusional?" I look back at Asha. "Or worse, what if she doesn't want me at all? What if she looks at me and she sees the weak woman I fear I am?"

Asha slips her arm around my waist, linking her hand with mine at the small of my back. "You are not weak. You never were. Those were the lies they told you. Because a woman who sees her power is a woman who cannot be controlled."

I lean into her. "Where do you summon that fortitude? You amaze me at every turn."

She blows out a breath. "I know I'm always the smartest person in the room. That helps."

I laugh. "By the gods, I love you, Asha. More than you'll ever know."

She squeezes my hand. "I love you too, Your Majesty."

"No," I say quickly. "Never again. We were always equals, you and I. Or maybe you were—"

"Stop," she says, knowing exactly where I'm going with that disparaging mark about myself.

"Okay. Yes. *Equals*."

She nods.

"And as equals, there are no titles. I am just Wendy. Forevermore."

"Well, it's a pleasure to meet you, Wendy. I'm Asha."

"Nice to meet you as well, Asha. I have a sense we'll be fast friends."

She laughs again. It's been a while since we've had this lightness between us. In Everland, we were always on high alert, always preparing for a betrayal or a coup or the outbreak of war.

I glance back out to the city, to the street across from our port, and immediately, my heart freezes.

I know that tall, blond, broad-shouldered man.

He's haunted my nightmares.

"Peter Pan," I breathe out. "He's here."

CHAPTER SIX

ROC

HE'S IN THE BALLROOM OF MADDRED MANOR.

There is music in the distance. A violinist playing a new arrangement of *Madame la Mort*. The notes are haunting. It reminds him of his mother.

There were two versions of Anjelaka Maddred: melancholy or manic.

If there was a third version of her, one that smiled or told secrets or danced or felt joy, he had never met her.

By the time he was born, she was a woman with glassy eyes and a heart of ash.

The tempo of the arrangement intensifies. It's the inner battle of *Madame la Mort*.

To live or to die? To love or be loved? To give a life for that love?

He follows the music.

Down the hall and past the gilded frames of past nobility. Past the library where his sister's piano sits, past the smoking room, the parlor.

The double doors are open to the garden beyond.

A shadow is in the middle of the boxwoods where the low-cut hedges form a Bone knot.

"Mother?" he calls.

She keeps playing, the moving bowstring catching a slant of waxing moonlight.

There is stillness in the garden. The air is misty, and it swirls around her willowy frame.

He crosses the garden to her and reaches out...

And she disintegrates into ash.

Someone laughs behind him.

He turns to find the witch.

"So pathetic." She claps slowly. Deliberately. "I never would have taken you for a mommy's boy."

He steels himself.

The music continues in the dark, now too far from his reach.

"What do you want?" he asks.

"I need you to come here."

"To my childhood home?"

She stares at him and says nothing.

Trapped in his body, in his mind, the witch is somehow sharper, more demon than woman. Her fingers are capped in black ink, her teeth stained red. She wears a black dress that has no silhouette, just shadow edges.

Her eyes are bright, though. Full of something he can only describe as *hunger*.

"I will not take you to Darkland," he tells her.

"Then I will make you devour everything you love."

She hangs her head back and laughs.

I AM SUDDENLY, ACHINGLY AWAKE.

I hear his breathing first.

The Captain shifts in the wingback chair. A scrape of fabric. A rattle of a watch chain.

Has he been keeping time for me? The man terrified of a ticking clock?

The flicker of candlelight gilds the Captain in gold, but it does nothing to hide the swollen underside of his eyes, the shadows that darken his skin.

I'm only vaguely aware of the destruction I have caused him, but I already know the price has been too high.

There is a sudden sinking feeling in my gut and I know right away what it is: *guilt*.

I quickly bury it.

The witch is always there ready to exploit a weakness and guilt is an emotion I cannot abide by. Not now. Not ever.

The Captain's eyes trail up my body and then settle on my face. There is a distance to his gaze, like he is lost in thought, and it takes him several seconds to realize I'm staring back.

He lurches out of his chair, pulls his pistol from its holster. His hand trembles a little. His breathing is shallow.

The ship sways, and the Captain stumbles. Proof that he is not himself. No one is more adept at the whims of the sea than Captain James Hook.

"Is it really you?" he asks, his voice thin, trembling.

It does not escape me, the fact he already has the pistol arm cocked, ready to shoot.

I don't tell him that a bullet will not stop me. I don't tell him that there is only one weapon in the Seven Isles capable of killing me and he doesn't have it. I think Smee does, though. How else would she have wounded Vane?

Did she ever tell the Captain?

"It's me." I close my eyes and take a breath. My heart is racing. My stomach is in knots.

I'm finding it difficult to tell the difference between dreams and nightmares and waking hours.

I never dream of my mother. Not anymore. But the accuracy of the dream...

My mother loved *Madame la Mort. Madame Death.*

My aunt Roan often told me that my mother came out of the womb a "melancholy child, obsessed with the darkness, always flirting with monsters."

Did she know Aaric Soren Maddred was a monster when she married him? Did she know she would birth monsters too?

"How long have I been out?" I ask the Captain.

"Several days."

The pistol still hangs mid-air between us.

The ship sways again, but it has the directionless sway of a harbor, not the sea.

"Neverland?" I ask.

"Yes." He finally uncocks the pistol. "We're docked. Asha has gone to the treehouse."

I sigh and scrub at my burning eyes. It feels like I've not slept at all. "What do you have to drink?"

The Captain holsters the pistol and turns a circle, then decides on a direction and goes to a half-drank bottle of rum. He pours me several fingers in a cut crystal glass and brings it back. His hand is still trembling. The dark liquor sloshes inside.

I meet his eyes.

"Did I hurt you?"

He blinks rapidly. "No."

"Wendy?"

"No."

I breathe out. Thank fucking god.

"Your crew?" I ask next.

His jaw clenches, and he says nothing.

"Anyone you care about?"

"Take the drink, Roc."

I don't often take his orders, but I make an exception now, aware that I am on thin ice.

I take the glass and pull myself into a sitting position, slinging it back in one gulp.

Ahhh yes. That's better.

The alcohol warms my throat and drives away some of the gnawing, never-ending hunger.

He returns to the wingback, some of the tension fading from his body.

He looks impossibly tired.

"How many?"

With his head leaning against the flared wing of the chair, he closes his eyes, inhales through his nose. "Six. We barely made it to the harbor. We're operating on a skeleton crew and half of those who remain want to throw me and you overboard."

I laugh.

The Captain sits upright. "It's not funny!"

"Well, it's a little funny. Do you even know how to swim?"

He glowers at me. "Of course I know how to swim!"

"Don't worry, Captain, I'll keep you afloat."

He stands abruptly, causing the chair to rock on its wooden legs. "Not even conscious five minutes and already you're harassing me."

"Five minutes? So you have been keeping time."

He goes still.

I meant it as another joke, but the anguish on his face says I've gone too far.

He is distressed and he has *been* distressed.

All because of me.

Rarely am I serious. Not anymore. Not since Lainey died.

But that look...

Like he could cry.

"How long?" I ask him.

His jaw clenches again and he takes a breath. "You've been...devouring every ten hours."

I curse beneath my breath.

"So it is bad?"

"We are not meant to shift multiple times in one day. One shift, one meal, should put me out for at least a day, usually two and we are warned not to devour again for weeks at the very least. Months would be better."

I glance up at him. "You once asked me why I kept time, why I didn't just shift and devour at my discretion."

"I remember." He swallows. "You told me there was a cost."

"Yes. It's not just the recovery period, the vulnerability in being unconscious. Too many shifts and..." I sink back against the headboard and close my eyes. "Too many shifts and a day will come when I can no longer shift back."

Silence grows thin between us. I have never told anyone this secret. What I am, what Vane is, we are not from this realm. No one in the Seven Isles has had to suffer the consequences of a permanent shift. Of a monster who cannot be stopped.

I open my eyes to find the Captain staring at me.

The anguish has returned, but it's different now, shadowed by fear.

"I won't let that happen," he says, his voice unwavering. "How do we fix it?"

I pull the tangled sheets away from my legs and put my feet to the ship's floor. I'm naked, apparently. Just as well.

"Clothes?" I ask. The Captain nods at a cabinet and I go to it, finding trousers, a button-up shirt. I start pulling on the pants when the room sways.

I didn't drink that much. I shouldn't be drunk already.

My stomach rolls and a shiver crawls up my spine.

"Bloody hell," the Captain says and staggers back.

I catch my reflection in the mirror over the washbasin.

My edges are fraying to purest black.

CHAPTER SEVEN

WENDY

Peter Pan emerges from the market street into the golden light of the docks. People bustle past him, keeping their eyes down, but they make sure to give him a wide berth.

Asha tightens her grip on my hand. "I have your back. No matter what."

"And if he's a god like the books say?" I whisper out of the corner of my mouth.

"Then we will go down together trying to kill a god. It will be an epic tale. There will be ballads."

I chuff out a breath, almost a laugh.

Peter Pan is at the head of the group. The rest of them form behind him, like a V of wolves.

He was always the leader. Everyone was always looking to Peter Pan for permission or acceptance or answers.

They cross the street that runs parallel to the harbor dock.

And then Peter Pan looks up and locks eyes with me. His steps falter.

"Oh," Asha says beside me. "Do you see that?"

"Is he—"

"You've disarmed him." Asha gives my hand another squeeze before pulling away. "This is good. Use that." Her hands go to her hips, where a dagger is strapped on either side.

Peter Pan comes to a stop in the middle of the cross street and the others come to a stop beside him.

And that's when I see her.

Winnie Darling.

"Wow," Asha breathes out. "She looks just like you."

I catch myself tearing up again.

Asha isn't wrong. Winnie Darling has the same thick, dark hair. Her's is a little longer than mine, and it's wild and untamed. Even though we've been at sea several days, having escaped a civil war, old habits die hard and I've been combing my hair every morning, twisting it into a chignon, careful to get every pin in its perfect place.

She's thinner than I am—are they feeding her?—but there's a strength to the line of her shoulders that reminds me of Asha. She's sure of who she is and what her place is among these feral boys.

Nothing seems to have changed about the Lost Boys.

Vane is next to Winnie, looking just as dark and dangerous as I remember.

On Pan's other side are twin brothers. Likely Kas and Bash, the fae princes. I was before their time. James informed me of them joining Pan, of warring with their sister, of reclaiming their wings.

"I'm going down," I tell Asha.

"You sure you don't want to make them come to you?"

If I stand here waiting any longer, I'm worried I may vibrate myself right off the quarterdeck. I'm full of energy that needs to be expended and I don't want my first meeting with my descendant to be shaky and sweaty.

"I'm sure."

Asha loaned me a pair of her leather trousers, but the old habit of lifting my skirts catches me off guard and I find my hands fumbling at my thighs. I quickly turn and make my way down the quarterdeck and to the gangplank.

Seeing the shifting sea beneath the gangplank has me doubting this decision. I don't love heights, and I especially don't love deep, dark water, but I take a breath and make the first step down, following the pattern of the toe boards to keep myself from slipping over the edge.

As soon as I'm on the stone of the harbor road, I feel better.

You can do this, Wendy.

Peter Pan doesn't matter.

He holds no power over you.

I step forward, teeth clenched together.

Winnie presses a hand to Pan's chest and he stops, looks down at her.

Her lips move, but I can't hear her words. We're still too far away.

Pan scowls at her. She scowls back and points at him, then at me.

Finally, he relents. He and the Lost Boys stay behind as Winnie comes forward alone.

Asha and I glance at one another.

"I don't think you have to worry about her," Asha mutters.

Did Winnie Darling just order Peter Pan to stay behind?

I love this girl, my distant descendant, already.

And seeing the way she's advocated for herself, how

she's handled Pan easily and without fighting, gives me confidence.

I step forward.

She quickens her pace.

My heart races in my chest and my stomach swims.

We meet at the edge of the road.

The people of the harbor continue their work around us, oblivious to the weight of this moment and what it means.

"Hi," Winnie says.

"Hello." It's taking everything inside of me not to burst into tears.

She holds out her hand. It's small, her fingers delicate. Her fingernails are painted a bright shade of pink. There is an acorn tattooed on the underside of her wrist.

A kiss.

I take her hand. Hers is cool, firm. Mine is clammy and unsure.

We have suffered the same curse and yet have found ourselves with different destinies.

"I'm so happy to meet you," she says and smiles up at me. She's shorter by a few inches. Tiny. Bird-like. But somehow strong.

"I...I..." My eyes are glassy. My nose is burning.

Winnie frowns and then suddenly she's hugging me, her arms tight, squeezing me.

"It's okay," she tells me. "You don't have to say anything. I'm so glad you're here."

I fall into the hug, my arms around her shoulders.

I wanted to show strength. I wanted to show I was unmarred by all of the years that spanned between Pan and me.

But there is only the truth.

I hug Winnie Darling fiercely and sob with relief.

PETER PAN AND THE LOST BOYS GIVE US A MOMENT ALONE. FOR that, I'm thankful.

I breathe in the scent of Winnie Darling and she immediately makes me think of the treehouse. Cloudberries and sweet tarts and salty ocean air.

This girl is my great-great-great something granddaughter and yet in my arms, she feels like a long-lost sister.

Breaking the hug, I find Asha beside me, an embroidered kerchief in her outstretched hand.

"Thank you." I take the offering and dry my face. "I'm sorry. I told myself I wouldn't cry and now here I am, crying."

I'm overwhelmingly relieved to be anywhere other than Everland.

I'm free but terrified of it all the same.

"You can cry," Winnie says, rubbing my arm. "You can scream or rave or dance if you'd like. No one will judge you after everything you've been through."

At the next dock, a porter shouts to his crew directing luggage and crates. In the distance, the lighthouse flickers on, the beam of light spinning through the growing darkness out to sea.

I catch movement beyond Winnie and see Pan and the Lost Boys coming our way.

"If your reunion is over," Pan says, "I'd like to know why the fuck—"

I step around Winnie, right up to Pan, and smack him across the face.

One of the twins, Bash, I think, snorts and turns away, trying to hide his reaction. Kas frowns at his brother, whispering a reproachful word.

Vane stands by, waiting.

Peter Pan barely moves. He probably felt only a fraction of the hit. Perhaps my hand is no more damaging than a tidal breeze.

But the satisfaction I feel...

His chest rises with a deep breath through his nose. Steeling himself.

He looks down at me.

My heart thuds beneath my ribs.

I expect him to toss me into the sea.

Instead, he says, "It is the least that I deserve for leaving you on Everland. But that is the only retribution you will get. Do you understand, Wendy Darling?"

It takes me several moments to process what he's saying as adrenaline courses through my veins.

He's letting me off with that?

It's not at all what I expected.

I summon all of the bravado I once needed while in the Everland Court. I pull on my queenly persona, give him a curt nod and say, "Very well."

Vane steps in front of Pan, dominating my line of sight. I have to take a step back. I've forgotten just how big Pan and the Lost Boys are. Everlanders are a much smaller people. Slight in frame, mostly under six feet. I feel like I've stepped into the land of giants.

"Where's Roc?" Vane asks.

"He's—"

There's a commotion behind us on the ship. We all turn to see James racing off the ship's deck, down the gangplank. "It's happening again!" he yells.

"What's happening?" Pan asks.

"Roc?" Vane says.

"He's turned—" James says just as the ship's starboard side explodes in a cloud of debris and a dark shadow flies into the night.

CHAPTER EIGHT

HOOK

On the dock, Peter Pan cuts me off.

"Where the fuck do you think you're going?"

For most of my life here on Neverland, I was consumed with the constant desire to destroy Peter Pan. Now, here he is within arm's length, close enough to gut with the sharp tine of my hook.

But now, none of that matters.

There is one driving need pounding in my chest: I have to get to Roc.

"He's going to devour your entire city if I don't get to him."

Vane grabs Pan by the bicep and pulls him back. "He's right. We don't have time for this shit." To me, he says, "Why did he let time run out? Was there no one for him to feed off of?"

Wendy and Asha and I share a look.

"What?" Vane says, catching our hesitancy.

"It's why we're here," Asha says.

"Roc can't control the turn," Wendy adds.

I don't know much about what Roc and Vane are—he's

been less than forthcoming about the particulars—but I can tell by the look on Vane's face now that he immediately knows what this means.

"What did he devour?" he asks.

"A witch," Wendy tells him.

"A Myth Maker witch," I clarify.

"Fuck." Vane turns a circle, his hand over his eyes, his jaw flexing with a grind of his teeth. "Fuck!"

Winnie tucks a lock of hair behind her ear as the wind picks up on the dock. "Share with the class. Why is this bad?"

"I know why he's come here." Vane drops his hand and starts off down the dock forcing us all to catch up to him.

"I second Darling," Bash says. "Care to share more?"

Vane follows the path that Roc took, his pace quick. "We rarely have control when we devour and sometimes we devour something we shouldn't. There is one rule we must abide by: do not devour power."

At the end of the harbor road, a row of shops leads inward to the heart of the city and further beyond, screams rent the air.

"Devouring power has..." Vane pauses and turns to Pan. "It has its consequences. A device was crafted to offset the mistake."

"What kind of device?" Kas asks as he ties his hair back.

"A hat."

Kas stills, his knot of hair only half done up. "Hold on... did you say a *hat*?"

"Yes, I said a fucking hat. The particulars don't matter."

"I think they do," Bash counters. "What kind of hat is it? A baseball hat? A cowboy hat? A bucket hat?"

Kas frowns at his brother. "What the fuck is a bucket hat?"

"I don't know, honestly. I just heard a mortal talking about them. I imagine it's a bucket you wear on your head."

Pan turns to the twins. "Will you two shut up?"

More screams fill the air. Impatience is beating at my temples. "Do you have this hat?" I ask.

Vane shakes his head. "It's not on Neverland."

"Then where?" Wendy asks.

Vane looks away. "It's on Darkland."

Bloody hell. We've come here for nothing. How much time does Roc have left before he can no longer turn back?

A gun is fired around the next street corner and a crowd goes running past the intersection.

"I can help him." I come to stand in front of Vane and Pan. "I've been able to talk him back into his form. Let me help."

"He's right." Wendy stands beside me. "He's been shifting rapidly for days. We know how to bring him down."

Pan scowls at us but quickly relents when another bullet is fired. "Fine. Kas and Bash, fly to the north. Vane?"

Vane is already following the sound of the commotion.

"Never mind," Pan mutters. To Winnie he says, "Fly back to the Treehouse and don't leave."

"Nice try." She snorts. "I'm not going."

"Darling," Pan growls.

"Don't Darling me," she says. "You need me and the shadow."

Wendy glances at her descendant with a new air of admiration. "Asha, Winnie and I will go around to the next street to try to hedge him in."

Pan doesn't argue, so apparently the Darlings hold the power now. I can't say I'm surprised. I am impressed, however. Good form, ladies. Good form indeed.

"And Hook—" Pan says.

"I'm not leaving him to you," I tell him, risking my neck and my head. "I'm going after him. He's my monster now."

Something changes in Pan's expression. It's almost imperceptible. A flicker of surprise.

"Do what you will then, Hook." Pan holds his arm out, gesturing me forward. "Don't let me hold you back."

Up until now, Roc hasn't hurt me. Every time he's come close, he's shifted back.

I hope now isn't the first where he proves me wrong.

WE ALL DISPERSE THROUGH THE CITY STREETS. I TURN DOWN THE nearest alley, following the sound of destruction two blocks up. A woman comes barreling out of a tavern carrying a chicken and a bag. She nearly slams right into me. "Get out of the way!" she yells and the chicken shrieks in her arms.

Up the next block, behind a row of trade shops, a door bursts open and three young men scramble out shouting at one another in a language of sharp constants and rolling Rs.

I continue forward, cautious.

Glass breaks somewhere inside the next building and in front of me, a man leaps out an open window. His knee gives out and he hits the cobblestone on his side before scrambling onto all fours and charging past me.

I peer in the open window. It's a woodworking shop with several pieces of large machinery where spindles are turned and boards sanded. A shadow darts past the window. A table is knocked over.

I go to the back door and try the latch, but it's locked from the inside.

At the weathered windowsill, I prop my good hand on it

and pop my head into the dim. "Roc," I call evenly, quietly so as not to alarm him.

The shadow again. A chair teeters on its back legs before slamming back to the floor.

"Roc. It's me. It's...*James.*"

His dark, shadowy form flies past me through the window, jumps off the next building before flying to the next intersection.

"Roc!"

I race after him.

He darts to the left, back toward the sea.

"Roc. Stop!"

More screams. I reach the intersection, and several fleeing citizens slam into me, spinning me around. My hook catches in a woman's blouse, and she comes to a yanking stop. She looks at my hook, then at me, and screams bloody fucking murder in my face.

"If you'll hold still..."

She keeps screaming, her round cheeks flush with adrenaline.

"Miss, please—" She slaps me. Continues screaming.

I manage to disentangle myself and once free, she darts off like a scared doe.

"Christ," I mutter, my cheek stinging, and hurry after Roc.

The street flows downhill, bordered on one side by a warehouse and the other by stone and timber apartments. At the bottom of the hill, now free of the harbor, the sea laps against the sandy shore. Several large rocky outcroppings border the alcove, creating a private beach for the row of apartments above.

I spot Roc across the beach in human form.

I exhale a breath of indescribable relief.

He's got his back propped against a boulder, and there's something moving on his lap.

Is that a kitten?

"Bloody hell." I race across the beach. The sand grabs at me, making it harder to find purchase with the soles of my boots.

Roc looks up, seeing me careening toward him. "Captain," he calls and smiles. He's bloodied, his shirt torn.

"Give me the kitten!" I screech, heart pounding in my ears.

Roc pulls the little ball of fluff to his chest and scratches at its ears. "Why? Is it a beast I've not met?"

"No. You're...*you*...give me the kitten before you eat it!" I come to a halt in front of him, kicking up sand.

Roc scowls at me, dusts the sand from his trousers. "Do you truly think so little of me?"

The cat nuzzles his chin, purring loudly. It's barely the size of Roc's hand, its eyes big and round and bright amber. It can't be much older than a month and two.

"Do you blame me for being wary? How many people did you just eat?"

There's a smear of blood on his face and a splatter of it across his torn shirt.

"Don't make me count my sins, Captain."

"I rest my case."

He cradles the kitten in his left hand and hoists it up in front of him, gazing into its eyes. "Don't listen to him. I would never eat you."

I sigh. "We have enough problems. Let the kitten go."

"Very well." Roc sets the kitten in the sand and slowly climbs to his feet. "Don't look so sullen, Captain. That was a quick shift. And now we're on Neverland and Vane will give me—"

"He doesn't have it."

Roc comes to a stop. "The hat?"

"It's not here."

There is no emotion on Roc's face, but the glint in his bright green eyes tells me enough. He's afraid.

"Where is it?"

"He said Darkland."

Roc turns away, his hands on his hips, his head bowed. His shoulders rise with a deep breath and I unconsciously step back, unsure of his state of mind.

This contraption, this hat, was his saving grace, and now we're even farther away from it. It'll take us at least six days to reach Darkland. I don't think I have crew enough to make the trip.

"I can't go to Darkland," he says, his back still to me.

"I know it's a long trip, but—"

He turns back to me. "The witch wants me to go."

This is the first time he's spoken of her directly. When he first shifted on my ship, after we escaped Everland, I thought I saw her face within his dark shadowy form. I thought my mind was playing tricks on me. After all, the witch was a specter from my past, a nightmare reminder of what my father had done to me. I thought perhaps her visage was still haunting me.

But no, if she's speaking to Roc, if she has some semblance of form within his monster, then she is not dead. It's not just her power harming Roc, she is as well.

"Why does she want you to return?"

"I don't know." He starts across the beach. The kitten meows at him and falls in line at his heel. "She showed me my childhood home and told me to return. I refused her. With the Remaldi line mostly gone, Darkland succession is likely in chaos and I..." He trails off and stops where the beach meets the road.

"You what?"

"It wouldn't be a good time for me to return."

"Why?"

The kitten sits back on its hind legs and paws at his trousers. He bends down to scoop it up and sets it on his shoulder like a parrot. "I guess we're keeping the kitten."

I scowl. "We are not keeping the kitten."

"How could you possibly turn away such an adorable creature?"

"Cats are beasts."

He flashes his teeth at me. "And? We both know you love beasts."

"They have claws. Claws ruin things."

Roc turns to it, its face just inches from his. "He'll come around," he tells the cat and starts up the hill.

"Roc."

He keeps walking.

"There are no cats allowed on my ship!"

But the cat remains a fixture on his shoulder as he continues up the street, and I'm not sure I have the energy to fight him.

"Bloody hell," I mutter. I guess we have a fucking cat.

CHAPTER NINE

VANE

There is carnage everywhere. It immediately takes me back to Darkland when Roc and I both embraced our beasts. We were always ready to devour. Anything and anyone who stood in our way. Back then we had nothing to lose. And we sure as fuck weren't concerned with the consequences.

Now I have things to protect. Now I have a life I actually like.

I round the corner of the wood shop and come face to face with my brother.

This, too, is a distant reminder of what we were together.

His clothing is torn. His face is bloody. But he's on his feet, conscious. Another indication that whatever is going on with him, it's not right. Usually after a devouring, we're out for hours, sometimes days. He shouldn't be coherent.

Hook stands beside him, his body tight, ready to fight me.

And there's an orange kitten on Roc's shoulder meowing loudly at me.

"Brother," Roc says.

There are a dozen things I want to say to him. Words I've never had the strength to give oxygen to.

He's come and gone on Neverland since I left our island, but we've never been as close as we were when we ruled the Darkland Umbrage. Before Lainey.

Our sister's death broke something between us.

Sometimes, when I allow myself grief, I mourn the loss of my brother just as much as my sister.

"I need to speak with you," Roc says.

"I know."

"Take him." He hands the kitten to Hook.

"What—" The kitten lands in the cradle of Hook's arm and then paws at the hook attached to his arm like it's a play toy. "What am I to do with it?"

"Pet it, Captain."

Roc starts down the nearest alley and disappears through an open door leading into the back of a bakery. Everyone has abandoned their work posts after his monster charged through, so we find no resistance to our intrusion.

He walks through the kitchen and beneath the archway leading to the bakery's front shop. There's a glass case full of fresh baked goods and several glass cloches on the counter displaying cakes and tarts. Beyond the counter are a handful of round tables.

Roc opens a cloche and plucks out two chocolate croissants, then plops down in a chair at the front window.

With the violence over, some of the townspeople have left their hiding spots to spill out into the street. Two men in overalls saunter past, their voices carrying through the cracked front door. They're complaining about Peter Pan bringing more trouble to the island.

I drop into the chair across from my brother as he bites into a croissant. The pastry crackles beneath his teeth.

"What did you get yourself into, Roc?" I ask.

He stretches out his long legs. "I need the hat."

"I don't have the hat."

He uses his index finger to scoop up a melted glob of chocolate from the open end of the pastry, then sucks it off his finger. "Why would you leave it on Darkland?"

"With the shadow, I can't devour. I had no need for it."

"Mmm." He nods, takes another bite. His gaze strays out the window where a woman picks up the basket she'd abandoned on the street when she fled the scene of Roc's destruction.

"Why did you devour a witch in the first place? You fucking know better."

"I was mad."

I snort. Once upon a time, back on Darkland, we were known as the Madd brothers. A shortening of our surname and an apt descriptor for our family and what we are or what we can become if we're not careful.

"I can't control it," he admits. "It's getting worse."

The first croissant is gone now. He's avoiding looking at me. My brother doesn't like to ask for help. I think in all the years I've known him, he's never asked for a favor. Not from me, not from anyone.

I get up and go to the bakery's kitchen. There's a block of knives by the worktable and I pull out a long, sharp blade. On a shelf above, I find a line of white tea cups and snatch one of those too.

When I return to the front, Roc looks up. At the shine of the blade, he grimaces.

"I don't want your blood."

"You'll fucking take it and shut the fuck up about it."

I set the teacup in front of him, then press the sharp tine of the blade to my wrist and pull. The shadow hisses at me and shrinks away from Winnie, surging toward me. It doesn't really speak to me, but the feeling I get when the power floods my veins is, *Whatever do you think you're doing?*

I sense Winnie coming to a stop wherever she is in the city.

I'm okay, I tell her, and the worry fades.

The first draw of the knife is nothing more than a scratch. The blade isn't special, just Winterlander steel, not magical enough to do real damage. I pull again and press harder.

My skin finally breaks, and a bead of blood wells up. I hold the wound over the teacup.

The flow of blood is slow, the cut not quite big enough.

A clock ticks above the counter behind us. A slow tick-tock that churns up dark memories and darker urges.

I haven't been a monster in years, not since I hunted down and claimed the Darkland shadow. Sometimes, what I was before, the things I did, it all feels like a fever dream.

When there's a finger of blood in the cup, Roc grabs it and quickly slings it back.

He didn't want it, but I know he needs it.

He slinks down in his chair, eyes closed once he's swallowed it down.

Our blood is meant only to be drunk when in dire need of stabilizing the monster. It's meant for emergencies only when nothing else will work.

It was Roc's blood that helped me through the first phase of claiming the Darkland Shadow. When it fought me at every turn, when it tore at me from the inside, leaving three bloody claw marks over my eye. My monster didn't like the shadow, and the shadow didn't like my monster, and the first night, I lay in bed, writhing against their warring, sweating through my clothes while my bones ached.

"Better?" I ask him, returning to the chair across from him.

His eyes snap open and his irises burn bright green. "Better."

Roc and I have seen each other at our worst. That is the one constant about our relationship. We will never turn away when our darkness shows its stains.

"You can't stay here," I tell him. "Peter Pan—"

"I don't want to stay here. Neverland's usefulness has run its course."

The clock keeps ticking.

"What will you do?"

"I have to go to Darkland." He looks over at me. "Will you come with?"

"No."

"Vane."

"No. I'm not going to Darkland."

He sits forward, his elbow propped on the table. He's serious now. He's rarely serious. Fine lines appear around his eyes as he frowns at me, his shoulders hunched forward. "Something is wrong."

"No shit."

"Not the witch. Not that."

I won't admit it to him, but he does have me slightly intrigued. "Then what?"

"The Myth Makers."

"The Lostland Secret Society?"

"Yes."

I sit up straighter. "Go on."

"I found a maker's mark on the back of the fae throne and another on the back of the king's bed in Everland."

Roc has been known to exaggerate a tale for the sake of the telling. But we don't lie about shit as serious as the Seven Isles Secret Societies. We're a part of one. We both know how serious this shit is.

"And the witch you devoured…"

"She told the Captain that a new myth rules the Council of Seven and that plans are in motion."

"What kind of plans?"

"I don't know and she won't tell me."

"Of course not." I drop back into the chair. "This isn't good."

"Now you know why I need that hat. I think…" He trails off and glances out the window again when Wendy, Winnie, and Asha appear in the street. They spot us through the glass and make their way over.

Roc lowers his voice, quickens his words. "I think the witch plans to use me. Think about it. The Lornes are dead. The Remaldis are dead. The Darkland line of succession is broken. Do you understand what I'm saying?"

"Our mother's line…"

"Yes."

The door opens and the bell above rings out. Wendy is first through the door, followed by Winnie and Asha.

"Where's James?" Wendy asks.

"Playing with a kitten," Roc answers.

"What?" She sounds a little mystified by this news.

Roc looks back at me. We could always speak to each other without using words. We aren't twins. There are three years between us. But monsters bound by blood can speak any language, even the language of silence.

I get up and turn to Winnie. "I'm going to Darkland."

"You're…what?" she says, a bit too quickly, a little high-pitched.

"Roc needs me."

She looks between me and my brother, then over at Wendy.

"You'll go too?" She asks her ancestor.

"Yes, of course. I'm not leaving Roc or James."

Winnie levels her shoulders. The shadow's power puffs up between us, sensing her digging in her heels. "Then I'm going."

"Absolutely not."

"You can't stop me."

"If I can't, then Pan will."

"He can't stop me either."

The shadow pulses like an energy field. It likes it when we fight because our fighting is always quickly followed by our fucking. And when we are together, no air, no space between us, the shadow is truly whole.

Wendy slips between us, her back to Winnie. It's been ages since I saw her last, but nothing has changed about her. Same dark hair, same big, round eyes. When Pan brought her to Neverland, she was a docile creature. Frightened by a thunderstorm. Wary of a shadow. There is still some reluctance about her, but I can tell new steel circles her spine.

"I want her to come," she tells me.

"You don't get a say," I remind her.

Winnie presses closer so that I'm now cornered by two Darling women. If one wasn't enough...

"I'm going." Winnie crosses her arms over her chest. Behind me, Roc laughs.

"You must know by now, brother, that it's a futile endeavor, arguing with a Darling."

The Neverland Shadow seems to echo this. I can feel it laughing at me. That fucker.

"Fine," I say, and Winnie's shoulders fall with relief. "But you follow my orders. You do not wander around on your own. And did I mention you will obey me?"

She angles a hip toward me as the shadow's energy dances. "Of course, Dark One. I will obey every word." She smiles innocently up at me.

Roc snorts. "We've no time for that. You two have bags to pack and I have a Captain to find."

"Asha and I will help," Wendy says.

"We'll meet back at the dock in an hour?" Roc asks me.

"Make it two. I'll have some convincing to do with Pan."

Roc nods. "I don't envy you that, little brother." Then he slaps me on the back and disappears out the back door with Wendy and Asha in tow.

CHAPTER TEN

WENDY

Because it was Roc who tore a hole through the side of James's ship, it's Roc who secures us a new vessel. We hire a charter ship with a larger crew and even finer accommodations. The chief stewardess, a woman twice my size with a long, black braid and bright red fingernails, shows me to my room below deck while we wait for Winnie and Vane.

She introduces herself as Maggie and compliments me on my trousers.

"I borrowed them, actually," I tell her. "I used to spend my days in complicated gowns, and it was…"

We pause at an intersection in the narrow hallways. She looks over at me, her dark brown eyes trained on me as if she's actually listening. What an odd feeling it is to feel like someone is interested in my answer for the answer's sake and not because they were pretending to be interested for court favor.

"It was what?" she coaxes.

"Insufferable," I admit.

"Ahh. Well, trousers suit you. I can tell you feel like yourself in them."

I glance down at the leather hugging my thighs. While they're Asha's pants, and very much the pants of a would-be assassin, of which I am not, I think Maggie might be right. I do feel more like myself.

"I appreciate your honesty and your kindness."

"Always a pleasure." She winks and continues down the hall. "Here we go." She opens the third door on the right with a small metal key.

"We call this the Lily Room. You can probably tell by the theme."

The room is large by ship standards with a queen bed draped in a thick duvet, on which are small, embroidered lilies. The curtains are a gauzy white that I imagine must billow with sea breeze when the window hatch is open.

There's a chair in the corner upholstered in rich indigo velvet. And beside it is a door leading to a small adjoining bathroom.

"If you need anything," Maggie says, "ask me or my second, Quin. Quin wears a red jacket signifying their position on the ship. They are the only person with that jacket so they are hard to miss."

"Okay. Got it."

"Anything above deck, ask the deckhand, Mr. Kepler. He looks like an old, crotchety fisherman, but he's nice enough." She smiles. "But take my advice, do not mention the Storm of Howel to him. He has about seven different tales about the storm, and you will never escape him."

I laugh. "Noted."

"Beyond that, we'll stay out of your way. This is your ship while on board."

With a nod, she hands me the key to my room and takes her leave.

I turn a tight circle, taking in the rest of the room. A few hooks are on the wall beside a small writing desk and an end table on one side of the bed with a clock and a lamp.

It's cozy and inviting. How Roc managed to pay for this, I will never know.

Slipping the key into my pants pocket, I leave the room and run right into Roc. The ship's halls are narrow even by my standards, and his shoulders nearly touch either side.

"Your Majesty," he says down to me.

"Stop."

"Only when I want." He smiles at me, eyes glinting as if he's suggesting something else entirely.

"You seem better."

"Vane's blood. It stabilizes me."

"Is that a long-term solution?"

"Not in the slightest."

"Oh. Well..."

Why am I so awkward around him?

He makes me nervous. He makes me want to run off the gangplank and sink into the dark water of the ocean and scream into the void.

Desiring Roc is not easy. And yet, it's the most primal thing I've ever felt. My attraction to him is like a seed planted long ago, fully in bloom now. A wild, sprawling thing with roots down deep.

"Well, I'm glad you're feeling better." I turn and start away.

"Where are you going?" he calls after me.

"To the upper deck."

"You're going the wrong way."

I come to a stop at the end of the hall and find a golden placard attached to the wall reading DINING with an arrow turning right.

I turn back.

Roc is leaning against the wall, his legs crossed at the ankle, arms crossed over his chest like a trickster god from a dark fairytale.

My heart kicks up.

He points in the opposite direction. "This way."

I switch directions, breezing past him, but he snatches me by the arm, pulling me to a stop.

In a blink, he has me pressed against the opposite wall, the line of his body against mine.

Our difference in height has the tattoo on his neck, the open mouth of a crocodile, right at my line of sight.

My swallow is loud between us, my heart thumping in my ears.

Since he and James arrived on Everland, we've only been together that once. But it hasn't stopped me from replaying it over and over in my head while heat burns between my legs and desire rises up my belly. I desire them both in different ways, for different reasons, but I wasn't sure if there would be more.

Roc and I were never alike. He was always sharp glass to my tender flesh. I'm not sure if we'll ever fit together in a way that isn't bloody and confusing. And while his relationship with James can sometimes be just as troublesome, they seem to have an understanding between them. A closeness I may never cross. I am jealous of them. I can see the time they've had without me, all the minutes and days adding up to a sum I can never hope to match.

I hadn't intended to have a serious conversation with him about anything. Not right now. Not while his monster wars with him. But the words spill out unbidden.

"I've been meaning to tell you...that if you love James more...if you would rather be with him than me then I will under—"

His hands take control of my body—one half wrapped around my throat, the other pressing at my opposite hip— and then he bends down and kisses me.

It is not a chaste kiss, but neither is it sensual. The way his mouth teases at mine, it's like another trick, like at any moment he could slip away.

Eyes closed, I lean into him, hungry for more of him, any amount he will give even if it breaks me.

His tongue meets me, a soft caress. Then he nips at my bottom lip and growls into my mouth.

"Shall I show you, Wendy Darling?"

"Is this what you came down here for?"

"I had no plan. No intentions." His fingers trail down my cheek. His touch makes my insides quake.

"I don't want your pity attention," I tell him, but the words come out wanting. Threaded with desire.

"Let me show you how I feel about you, Wendy Darling." His hand sinks to my thigh, then trails back up, slowly, achingly slowly, to the seam where my thigh meets my center.

I breathe out in a hiss.

"Just you and me," he goes on, his fingers brushing against my pussy, then gone just as quickly. "If we're to do this, the three of us, it must be explicitly clear that you both have me equally. I like to share. It's my favorite thing in the world. I want the Captain's cock in my mouth and my cock in your pussy and I want to hear you both moan as you come for me." His touch trails up and up, thumb brushing over my peaked nipple. "I have no time for jealousy. And certainly not *pity*."

He steps back, and the sudden absence of his body, and his touch, makes me pitch forward, my eyes popping open.

He's leaning against the wall again, smiling at me with a flash of his sharp incisors. "Okay?"

I swallow again, my body aching for him, my breath short. "Okay."

"Good."

A mewling sounds from the floor.

It's the kitten Roc seems to have acquired.

"Firecracker," he says and scoops the cat into his arms. "I wondered where you ran off to." He scratches the cat beneath the chin and the cat's eyes slip closed, nuzzling into his touch. "Come, my Darling girl. I'm told we're about to set sail and dinner will be served in an hour and ten. Which is just as well. I'm famished. And if I'm to pound that pussy later, I'll need all the strength I can get."

Firecracker in hand, he turns toward the upper decks, cooing to the cat as he goes.

WE'VE BEEN AT SEA NOW JUST AN HOUR AND A HALF, AND WE'RE all in the starboard side dining room. It's hard to imagine that in just a few days, I've shed my crown, found myself with James and Roc, and on Neverland again, meeting my Darling descendant.

I watch Winnie across the dining table. She's sitting between Vane and Asha, but her chair is inches closer to Vane. So close I imagine their knees are touching below the table. I've tried not to stare at them, but it's hard not to be curious and maybe a little envious. There is an ease between them that is unfamiliar to me. When I was on Neverland, everything about Vane was coarse and sharp. He was more likely to scowl at me than offer a kind word so I kept my distance.

When I heard his brother was arriving at the treehouse, I thought surely he must be cut from the same cloth. I was determined to hate Roc immediately. I was determined to make myself small and invisible because two scowling, cleaving men with unknown power was more than I could bear.

But then Roc walked in the door and the energy changed. He was tall, black-haired, and handsome, but somehow his presence felt like warm sunlight on chilled skin.

He was jovial, funny, always up for a good time. I was drawn to him.

Looking back, I can see I was desperate not to feel so afraid on Neverland. I had been taken from my home, told I held the key to finding Pan's shadow, of which I had no knowledge about. I couldn't fix Pan's plight and if I couldn't fix it, then I was useless and if I was useless...what would he do with me?

With Roc, I felt protected. Safe. Maybe it was naive but I did.

And while we're rebuilding on a shaky foundation, I still feel safe with him.

I just never expected to fight for his attention with James. Roc's earlier comment about sharing, about detesting jealousy has me examining it from all directions. I am jealous. I'm jealous of everyone's love. For the last however many decades, I've been alone, fighting for my place, trying not to get banished, killed, or imprisoned again.

I distrust everyone. Or at least I did, until Asha.

But the number of people in my life has tripled in a matter of days. I don't know how to let any of them in without exposing myself to more heartache.

I want what Vane and Winnie have.

But I want it with James and Roc and I don't want to be afraid of feeling less than between them.

How the hell do I do that?

Winnie looks up as if she can sense my internal distress. She frowns over at me. There's a gilded candelabra between us that holds three ivory candles. The flames flicker, the wax dripping down the sticks.

"Are you okay?" Her mouth moves, but the words are buried beneath the din of conversation between Vane, Roc, and Asha.

I give her a nod, even though it's half-hearted.

Beside me, James lurches in his chair and he cuts his gaze across the table to Winnie. She's staring back at him, eyes wide.

James turns to me. "You aren't eating."

I think she must have kicked him beneath the table.

I should be the one looking out for her, not the other way around.

I pick up my fork. "I am."

Maggie and her crew have prepared roasted chicken, potatoes, and broccoli. I break a potato in half and take a bit. "See?"

James leans into me, his hand on my thigh and my heart races to my throat. "I know this is strange. I know you've barely had time to process all of this. There will come a day when we are no longer putting out fires."

I smile up at him. There is earnestness in his expression. James was always a gentle breeze. The kind you lean into with a sigh.

"I'm looking forward to the day."

"Wendy," Roc says, and James and I pull apart.

"Hmm?"

"Your girl is trying to pry into my past with a knife. Is she always this forward?"

Asha is situated between Vane and Roc across the table from me. I meet her gaze. She's not uncomfortable being put on the spot. Asha has always liked a challenge.

"Yes," I answer.

"Well I don't like it," Roc answers, but he's smiling like maybe he does.

"I spent years in the Darkland Archives," Asha says, taking up her glass of wine. "You must know your origins are heavily censored, which makes you confounding and astonishingly interesting all at the same time."

"Do you hear that, brother?" Roc glances down the table at Vane. "We are astonishingly interesting."

"That's an understatement," Winnie answers.

"Do you know what they are?" I blurt.

The table goes quiet.

James squeezes my thigh beneath the tablecloth, almost a warning.

I turn away from them, suddenly embarrassed. "Sorry," I mutter. "I didn't mean to pry..."

"I don't know," Winnie answers. "Not entirely."

Roc and Vane share a look. Vane gives his older brother an almost imperceptible shake of his head.

Whatever they are, it leads me to believe it's rooted in some actual mythology, something we would recognize if we heard it. Asha's theory is Roc and Vane, or at least their ancestors, are not from the Seven Isles. I've spent enough time with her in the private palace library listening to her read myths and sagas, to know that the Seven Isles and my home world are just two of many. So it stands to reason that someone further back in Roc and Vane's line, or maybe even Roc and Vane themselves, crossed worlds just like

Peter Pan did to mine. Time and clocks didn't exist before the Bone Society, which means here, in the Isles, no one had a need for it until they did.

"What else did you learn in the Archives?" Roc asks Asha.

She sips from her wine glass while she contemplates the question. Asha has never been a person in a rush to speak. Sometimes there are long pauses between her answers while she digs through the archive of her mind looking for the best response.

"Vane's name is his birth name, but you weren't born a crocodile," she finally says.

"No." Roc smiles. "No, I was not."

"But your birth name doesn't appear at all. Not once."

Their gazes catch on one another like sand burrs on cloth.

"Are you asking me a question?" Roc says.

"What's your true name?"

"The only person alive who knows my true name is my brother and my uncle."

"Wait," Winnie says, turning to Vane. "You have an uncle?"

The line of Vane's lower jaw tenses as he scowls at Roc, clearly thinking he's said too much.

I didn't know they had an uncle. I thought most of their family was dead.

Roc rests his elbows on the table and leans toward Asha. Asha, for her part, does not move despite the tension in the air. "I assure you, Bonescar, my name is not as interesting as my monster. Perhaps next time I shift, I'll—"

I stand up so fast that my chair tips over and slams into the hardwood floor. Everyone turns to me.

"Don't, Roc. Don't ever threaten her."

He takes in a long breath through his nose, his chest expanding slowly and deliberately. "Fine. I'll pinkie promise. But not until she promises to leave my past in the past."

I'm not sure Asha can turn off her inquiring mind any more than Roc can turn off his monster, but Asha says, "I promise," anyway, because she's smart, and she knows when a lie is more important than the truth.

Roc holds out his pinkie to her.

Asha sits upright. "Is that necessary?"

"Of course. It's the most sacred promise of all."

With a disgruntled sigh, Asha hooks her pinkie finger around his and Roc gives their hands one hearty pump.

"There. It's settled."

"Thank you," I tell them both, but the look Asha gives me says she will not honor that pinkie promise, no matter how sacred Roc seems to think it is. Because he made a mistake: he revealed the fact that he possesses a secret, one he was willing to fight over.

Asha will never let it go.

CHAPTER ELEVEN

ROC

Once the dinner plates are cleared, and the others indulge in the dessert course, I saunter away from the room feeling disgruntled and still hungry despite the mountain of food I took down.

I open the door to the portside deck and the sea breeze wends in, tossing my hair in my face.

I rake it back as I head into the wind and find a folding deck chair open at the railing.

I sit and watch the stars move past.

This ship is faster than the Captain's. We'll be to Dark-land in no time at all.

The thought makes my head pound.

Leaning back, boot propped on the deck railing, I close my eyes and revel in the cool saltiness of the ocean air.

"Here."

I open my eyes. I didn't even hear Vane approach.

There's a wine glass in his hand, a swallow of blood pooling in the bottom.

"Dear brother, you shouldn't have."

"Take the fucking blood, Roc."

I lose control of my monster and suddenly everyone is bossing me around.

The blood sloshes when I snatch the glass from Vane, then drink it down in one gulp. His blood has the bitterness of shadow but the sweet warmth of our monster. I never stopped to question whether or not more power—power from the Neverland Dark Shadow—would be another mistake made. I don't have any room for hesitancy. Not now.

Vane drops into the chair beside me and folds his hands over his middle. "They're going to find out eventually."

"I know that."

"Asha is…"

"Something else."

Vane laughs. "She might be the most intuitive, intelligent person I've ever met."

"She's trouble."

He laughs again and looks over at me. "Are you scared of her?"

"Slightly." I smile. "Don't tell."

The silence stretches another moment.

"Did you scrub your existence from the archives?"

It's dark out here on the deck. We're sailing into midnight and only a glass lantern glows further down the deck. But even in the darkness, I can make out my brother's face. We have the same Maddred jawline, sharp and arrogant, the same noble nose that we inherited from our mother, the same dark brow. But his face is marred by scars. Mine is as handsome as ever.

When I don't answer him directly, he finds the answer himself. "Why?" he asks.

"I didn't want to be defined by what we are. I wanted to be defined by who I actually am."

"We are the monster and the monster is us. There is no separation between the two."

"Isn't there? You haven't shifted in years. You're less and less monster every day."

He snorts. "I still feel it sometimes slinking beneath the surface. Some days, I wake up dreaming of blood."

Laughter sounds in the dining room behind us, then the clinking of a glass.

I pull a cigarette from the pouch and offer Vane one. I light his first, then mine.

The sea air catches the smoke and shoots it across the deck.

With an exhale, I look over at Vane. "Did you ever think about going back to Darkland?"

"No. I didn't have a reason to return. Neverland is my home now."

"And your Darling girl?"

He keeps his gaze on the moonlit horizon, but I don't think he's looking at the ocean. "After Lainey, I didn't think I'd love anything ever again. Win taught me otherwise."

"This is the moment where I'm supposed to say something profound. Where I'm to remind you that the heart mends."

He glances over at me, the burning cigarette trapped between his knuckles. "But you won't. Because you don't believe it."

I sigh and take another hit. "Wendy and the Captain..."

"You're holding them at arm's length just like you did me. I know what you're doing. You don't have to try to find words to explain it because I already know you're going to downplay it. You want to be happy again? Grab them by the shirt and embrace them. And don't ever let go."

I search for a joke, something to deflect.

But words escape me.

I take a hit instead and then flick the spent cigarette over the railing into the ocean.

My exhale is heavy and smoke-laden.

"I never would have expected to receive relationship advice from you."

"And I never expected you to be fucking Hook and yet..."

I shrug. "What can I say? I have a thing for mouthy pirates."

He stands up and flicks his cigarette too, blowing out the last breath of smoke before opening the door. "I'm going to bed. You'll be good for blood for the rest of the night?"

"I think so."

"If you need me, come find me. Don't risk it."

"Yes, father."

"Shut the fuck up. Just listen to me for once." He disappears back inside, shutting the door behind him.

I stay on the deck longer, enjoying the night breeze.

WHEN I COME BACK IN, I FIND THE DINING ROOM EMPTY SAVE FOR Wendy. She's nursing the last of a glass of wine.

"I waited for you," she tells me and then laughs.

"Are you drunk?"

"I think so."

"Where's the Captain?"

"Apparently he heard the deck crew was having trouble with a sail or knot or something, so he—"

"Couldn't help himself."

"Precisely."

She laughs again and raises the glass to her lips.

I quickly snatch it from her grip and drink it back.

"Roc! That's mine."

The wine is dry and sweet. If I had to guess, it's a blend from Summerland. The berries grow fat and juicy on their vines.

"And now it's mine." I set the glass down. "You've had enough. Come." I offer her my hand. She scowls at me.

"I was once a queen, you know. I don't have to take orders from you."

My hand hangs between us.

I wait. I can be patient.

She doesn't have to take my orders, but she will. Just like with the Captain, I give them orders, they obey. It's the natural order of things.

She gives in, slipping her hand into mine.

On her feet, the ocean rises carrying the ship with it, and Wendy careens into my side. I wrap my arm around her, steadying her against my hip. She's warm and tiny in my grip, but she's not small. She's got all the right curves for my hands to roam, my tongue to paint.

When we were together, it was the Captain I was fucking. It's been many, many moons since I've felt Wendy Darling wrapped around my cock.

"Off to bed with you."

"With me? Or with you?" She gazes up at me, eyes glassy in the flickering lamplight.

"I'm not going to take advantage of you."

"Then let me take advantage of *you*."

"Naughty, naughty Darling girl."

I lead her down the hall to her room. A kerosene lamp is lit on her bedside table, casting deep shadows in her room. The bed is turned down. This ship, the Hannah Maria, is no royal ship, but they treat it like one, and I feel right at home.

Wendy stumbles into the room and starts unbuttoning her shirt. I remain in the open doorway, caught between temptation and good taste. The witch has been quiet since Vane shared his blood, but I can still feel her prowling in the darkness, urging me to sink into indecency.

"Wendy Darling," I warn.

"I'm not as drunk as you'd think." She slips out of the shirt, leaving her in leather trousers and a lace camisole, the thin material a whisper over her breasts, more a suggestion of clothing than actual clothing.

She takes a step toward me, the flickering lamp light dancing over her skin, highlighting the goosebumps running down her arms.

I meant what I said earlier, that I wanted to fuck her to show her she's mine. But every step she takes, I feel less and less like I'm the one in charge, and instead like the one being hunted.

She leans against the wall and arches her back a little so her breasts press against the camisole.

I shift directly across from her in the narrow hall leading into her bedroom. We are inches apart now, face to face.

"I have to tell you a confession," she says, her voice low.

"Go on."

"I am jealous."

"I know."

Her arms come up over her chest as if she means to shrink in size, to hide in plain sight. She's bearing her soul and cannot stand bearing her body at the same time.

"Do you remember what you told me? Why you took James's hand?"

I don't like talking about my single greatest regret.

"Yes," I answer.

She waits, then huffs out, clearly expecting me to parrot the answer back to her. But I won't.

"You said you cut off his hand because his hand touched what was yours."

"You," I supply.

"Yes."

"What are you getting at, Your Majesty?"

"Did you ever have feelings for me? Or was it just a game? Was I just property to claim?"

So we're going down that road.

"I could ask you the same. Back on Neverland, you leapt from my bed to the Captain's with very little restraint. And in the end, you chose neither of us. So is it wrong of us to find solace in one another?"

She scowls up at me, her arms tighter over her chest. "Solace. You fight him at every turn."

"Because I like it when he gets bratty. What are you getting at?" I repeat.

"I don't know. I don't want to be jealous. I want you to reassure me. I want you to tell me that I'm not just a bonus piece of candy, that I'm something more than a chess piece, a game to be won and—"

I close the rest of the distance between us, hook my hands beneath her thighs and hoist her up into my arms, slamming her against the wall.

She lets out a startled little gasp, but I swallow it with my mouth, tasting her wholly and completely with my mouth, my tongue, my fucking soul.

If she wants to doubt my intentions, I will show her instead.

She moans into me, wiggling her center against my crotch.

The heat of her pussy is impossible to ignore.

"Tell me," she says between gasps. "Promise me."

"I am moved by very little, Wendy Darling." I sink to her jawline, kissing down her neck. "I wouldn't have crossed an ocean to find you if you were nothing more than a game."

"Do you love us both?"

I nip at her ear and she hisses.

"I don't know if I'm capable of love anymore."

My brother's advice replays in my head.

But I don't want to think about love. Or contemplate the consequences of losing what is loved.

I just want to feel.

Pleasure and lust and temptation are close enough and I know pleasure like I know the sunlight. It's familiar and warm and I don't have to worry about it abandoning me. It's always there.

I let my tongue trail down the sensitive flesh beneath Wendy's ear and she wriggles in my grip. "Whatever I'm capable of, you will have it. That's my promise."

With her fingers threaded through my hair, she pulls my mouth back up to hers and kisses me. Her tongue is warm and soft and I sink into her.

"I'm not drunk. *Enough*," she adds between gasps. "Fuck me."

Legs wrapped around my hips, I turn her away from the wall and carry her to the bed, dropping her onto the mattress. The bed bounces. Wendy fights with the button on her trousers as I yank off her boots, then grip the pants by the cuffs.

I yank them from her legs and toss them aside.

She rocks up on her knees and takes a fistful of my shirt, tearing upward, pulling it over my head.

When my chest is bare, she runs her hands down my

pecs, then my abs, her wet lips trailing behind the caress of her fingers.

I hang my head back and breathe out, eyes closed.

Her touch is soft but electric. The touch of a feather and a lightning bolt.

My stomach tightens, and the pressure sinks to my cock.

I want to descend into the feel of her.

Her mouth grazes over my crotch where I strain against the material.

I straighten and look down, meeting her doe eyes.

She isn't innocent. She never was. I think someone once told her she needed to be, that to be a lady, she must be chaste and innocent. But there isn't an innocent bone in Wendy Darling's body. The sooner she learns that, the sooner she will be free.

I undo the latch on my belt and yank it from the belt loops with a yank, the leather snapping.

She undoes the button, the zipper, then frees me.

"Fuck," I hiss out.

She strokes me from base to tip, then sits forward on her knees, circling me with the soft pad of her tongue.

I won't last. I won't fucking last.

Hand buried in her hair, I guide her over the length of my cock. She moans against me, the hum sending shock-waves through my gut.

Maybe this is love. Maybe love is the same as worship.

We could all learn a thing or two on our knees.

When precum leaks from my dick, Wendy pulls back and swipes the tip of her tongue over it.

She may be the one in a position of supplication, but she holds the power over me. She always did.

She's worried I don't want her, not as much as the Captain, but I can't imagine being anywhere else.

I would cross not one ocean but a realm for her.

I coax her around to all fours and cover her backside with my body. My cock presses into her damp panties and she moans beneath me.

"Get up to the headboard," I order and she crawls up the length of the bed, placing her hands on the carved spindles.

I can smell her desire permeating the air.

With her back bent, I slip my hand up between her thighs, then around the seam of her panties to her soaking wet cunt.

Her moan is loud and high-pitched.

I slide up to her clit and make slow, deliberate circles.

Her ass sinks back, her body making an S curve, her hands still locked on the headboard.

Her breathing is shallow and fast.

I sense her cresting the edge.

Not yet.

I tear the delicate material of her panties from her body, exposing her pussy and sink my cock into her slick, warm wetness.

CHAPTER TWELVE

WENDY

Roc fills me up and I gasp out. I had forgotten what it felt like to be fucked by a monster.

His left hand comes up to my wrist, wrapping around me as he pumps into me. With every thrust, I sense him giving in more and more until we are just two beings chasing something more than physical pleasure.

I had it wrong—Roc and I are more alike than I thought. We are deep, dark water wishing to be free of a dam.

We are a tidal wave—*unleash me.*

He fucks me harder. Harder. His breathing is labored at my ear, his body covering mine.

The headboard slams against the wall. Again and again and again.

Roc's right hand snakes around my hip, his fingers sliding over my buzzing clit. I'm dripping wet and so fucking close I might scream.

I push back against him, sinking him deeper and he loses it, grunting into me, filling me up.

My own pleasure builds and builds and then the ocean wave crests.

My body tenses up, curls forward and Roc tightens his grip on my wrist, holds his fingers to my clit, forcing me to jolt through the aftershock again and again.

I breathe out, muscles blinking, causing me to shiver beneath Roc's warm body.

He lets go of my wrist, then coaxes me down to the bed.

I practically melt into the soft mattress.

Roc slips away, disappearing into the bathroom, and returns with a damp cloth. "Open up." He pushes my knees apart.

In the flickering light of the lamp, he looks dark and dangerous, like a shadow honed into a blade. But the way he takes care of me, tenderly, and gently, contradicts everything.

He told me he didn't think he could love, but I can't imagine any action more loving than this.

Satisfied, he returns to the bathroom to drop the cloth, then climbs into bed beside me, his back propped against the mountain of pillows. He tucks me into the crook of his arm, then pulls the duvet up and around me, ensconcing me in warmth.

The sheets are crisp. His body is mine. And I don't think I've ever felt so safe in a bed. Not in a long, long time.

My head resting on his chest, I can hear the steady beat of his heart.

It's the most honest thing about him. The part of him that is man and not some myth.

I want to be held by him like this always. He and James both.

Perhaps that makes me selfish, wanting both men, wanting them to declare their love. But I've lived too long under tyranny to demand anything less.

"Thank you," I say, my voice sleepy and far away.

His fingers trail through my hair. "Don't thank me yet."

It's a warning, sure, but beneath that, I hear his worry.

I think he's afraid of disappointing us. I think he's afraid of just how monstrous he may become.

CHAPTER THIRTEEN

HOOK

I can't seem to shake this cat. It's following me everywhere, mewling for treats, batting at my trousers as I pass, begging for attention.

"Go on, beast," I tell it as I make my way below decks.

But the beast either doesn't understand or pretends it doesn't.

I go to my room first, but find it empty and a little thread of disappointment pulls at my spine.

No matter. I shouldn't be surprised that the Crocodile has found other things to entertain himself while I was helping the crew untangle a knot.

I go to Wendy's room next.

The lamp has been turned down, but moonlight spills in through the circular window next to the bed.

Roc is there, his back propped against the headboard, Wendy curled in his arms. Roc is awake. Wendy is fast asleep.

The kitten meows, then charges in ahead of me, leaping onto the bed.

"There's my little firecracker," Roc whispers, cooing at

the beast. It clumsily makes its way up Roc's thighs, then finds a nest between Roc and Wendy, curling into them.

"Of course now it's behaving!"

"Shhh," Roc says, scratching at the cat's head. "He's sleepy, Captain. Let our firecracker rest."

I grumble. "Is Wendy..."

"She's all right. She needed reassurance."

I understand that more than I'd like to admit.

"Get over here," he orders.

I kick off my boots, shrug out of my coat, and toss it into the nearby chair.

There's just enough room on the bed to slide in on Wendy's other side, sandwiching her between us. She's warm and soft and smells like honeysuckle. If she needed further reassurance, I wish she would have come to me. I think we are both afraid of drowning in the Crocodile's ocean. I want her to know she is not alone.

Every day I'm shocked I'm still here, falling further and further in l—

"Did you save the ship?" Roc asks, teasing me.

"I like to make myself useful."

He smiles at me over the top of Wendy's head. "I always have a use for you, Captain."

"Poor form," I whisper, but I'm only half joking.

He chuckles to himself and Wendy stirs, moaning in her sleep. The kitten lifts its head, scowling at me as if it's my fault it's been disturbed.

"Has she been reassured?" I ask, tucking a stray hair behind Wendy's ear.

"I believe I did my part." His teeth flash in the moonlight.

"Poor *form*," I repeat.

"Oh Captain, my form was impeccable."

"Will you two shut up," Wendy murmurs, and then adds, "His form *was* impeccable."

"See?" Roc raises his brows at me.

"Don't feed his ego." Knowing she's awake, I relax my body into her, readjusting so she's half in my arms. She arches, sinking into me.

I never would have expected this to be our outcome, the three of us in bed together. We haven't spoken of where we go from here. We never had the chance.

I'm afraid to ask.

Just the thought of it has my heart racing beneath my ribs, my stomach see-sawing.

Roc looks over at me, his brow now furrowed.

"What is it?" he asks.

Wendy lifts her head to look over at me.

I swallow.

"You've reassured Wendy."

She readjusts so she can see me better in the sliver of moonlight.

"And—"

Wendy slips her hand into mine and squeezes.

"I know you don't like to stay in one place for long," I say. "I just need to know, after Darkland, after we fix you and you are well, will you leave again?"

I hate that Wendy and I are like sycophants for the Crocodile, on our knees begging for him to love us. I don't blame him for it. I don't think he wants us to worship him any more than he wants to be worshipped.

That's the problem—the Crocodile has always been free to roam. He's never owed anyone anything, not after he lost his sister and his brother.

I glance at him in the semi-darkness.

For the first time, I see real fear and suddenly I know...

he's held himself back all these years, claiming no one, not in any real way, to protect himself.

I can sense him retreating behind those walls, afraid to lose something, afraid to be lost in something.

Wendy and I are both staring at him now, waiting.

The stillness makes my stomach hurt.

Suddenly he's up and moving.

"Roc," Wendy says.

But he's gone in a flash, shutting the door behind him.

CHAPTER FOURTEEN

ROC

Yes, take them, the witch says. Claim them and use them and then devour them and we will all be together for an eternity.

I rush out a door on the starboard side of the ship.

All of the lanterns are off, the ship plunged in darkness save for its running lights and the distant flickering of starlight.

There is ocean stretching to the horizon on either side.

Endless darkness.

I collapse into a deck chair, head in my hands.

I suck in several deep breaths as white light blinks behind my closed lids.

I let my guard down and I could sense the witch seizing on my vulnerabilities.

She is always there, devouring me from the inside. She knows everything I want, everything I desire, and everything that terrifies me and she will use it against me.

I can feel her pressing against my insides, trying to force the monster out.

Devour them, she says again.

Devour them whole.

My stomach churns as the ship crests a wave.

Fucking hell.

I shouldn't have brought them. I shouldn't have brought them to Darkland where everything I've ever loved has died or gone.

Because now the witch knows that Wendy and the Captain...

I grit my teeth and lean back.

The witch knows how I feel...

Fuck.

I stand up, grab the deck chair by its back rail, and heave it into the ocean.

It hits the water with a splash and quickly sinks below the surface.

"Feel better?"

I look up to see Asha hiding in the shadows. I didn't even hear her come up.

Shows just how fucked I am.

"Minimally," I admit.

"Here." She emerges from the darkness and offers me a clay mug with a dark liquid inside.

"What is it?"

"It's a tea blend. My mother used to make it for me to calm my nerves."

"Do you have nerves that need to be calmed right now?"

She shrugs. "We're stuck on a ship with a man who won't tell us what kind of beast he is, whose beast continues to take over and devour people bone by bone. So, *a little.*"

I like this girl more and more.

I take the mug and sip from it. It's sweet and earthy, with a hint of floral.

"I think you already know what kind of beast I am," I say, handing the drink back.

She crosses one arm over her middle, using it to prop up the opposite elbow, mug held aloft as she contemplates me. "I do have a theory."

"And?"

"Still working. I will admit I am a scholar first, and a soldier second. Killing men was a necessary skill and I'm very good at it. But research, studying, translating, that's what lights my soul on fire. And your past is interesting."

"Mmmm. I think you're giving me more credit than I'm due. My past does not matter."

She laughs. "I think it's the only thing that matters. Not just *what* you are, but *who* you are."

My gaze cuts to hers. *She knows.*

"I left all of that behind a long time ago."

"But has it left you?"

I take the drink from her again and down another swig. The tea is good and, surprisingly, calming. "Have you told anyone?"

"I don't discuss theories, only facts."

Meaning she hasn't confirmed her suspicions with proof.

I give the mug back. "Do you have a theory about the witch?"

Asha goes to the railing and leans her back into it, the moonlight skimming her dark hair with strokes of silver. She's wearing all black with a dagger strapped to her waist. "Let me ask you this, can what you devour hijack you entirely? Permanently?"

I sigh. "Never been proven. But this thing happening with the witch leads me to believe it's possible."

"Then yes, I do have a theory."

I join her at the railing but prop my arms on the wrought iron and peer down at the churning ocean. "We have the same theory?"

"I think we do."

I'm desperate to get away from this conversation or at least turn the tides away from me. I don't like digging into my past. And I sure as hell don't like thinking about my future. Not when it's fucked.

"It occurred to me recently," I say, "that you might be the age of someone who was around during the worst of the Kimura coup in the remote Winterland Alps."

I don't have to look at her to sense how she goes rigid.

"A girl your age, she might have been, what, nineteen, twenty, when the revolt began?" I glance at her.

Her jaw is locked, her nostrils flared. "Eighteen," she corrects.

"Ahhh yes. The age a girl might be when she ascends to the Taira throne." I half turn to her. "The age a girl might be on her wedding night when the man she just married kills her entire family and steals her throne."

She swallows.

"I have my own theories," I tell her.

I don't miss the glassiness in her eyes. The way she doesn't move yet vibrates with rage.

"You know a thing or two about running," I guess. "So you understand why I'm reluctant to run back."

She sucks in a long breath through her nose, takes a step closer to me. A risky thing, inching toward a monster. I respect her boldness.

"I'm not reluctant to run back," she says, and then, with

a grit of her teeth, adds, "I am honing myself like a blade. Hands strong enough to kill. A mind strong enough to trick. I'm waiting for the day when he thinks he is safe. And then I will corrode him and his court, day by day, act by act. And when he has descended into paranoia, given in to the chaos I have sown, I will slip inside his bedroom—*my bedroom*—and I will jam my blade into his throat."

I smile over at her. "I admire the gentleness of your plan."

She rocks back, frowning at me, and then she laughs. "I haven't told anyone that plan. I've been afraid they'd tell me I'm crazy. Violent. *Mad.*"

I lean over. "Let me tell you a secret: we're all mad."

She laughs and rolls her eyes. "I suppose you're right, *Madd brother.*"

"So you do know more than you've let on."

"Of course."

"Do you know who my mother is?"

"Another theory."

"You know who my uncle is?"

"Yes."

"Then you have all the dots. Now connect them."

"I think you know I already have."

I push away from the railing. "Don't tell them yet. Let me find out what we're walking into on Darkland. I don't want them to get caught in the middle if I can avoid it."

She nods. "You'll keep my past between us?"

"I'm not much for gossip. Would you like to pinkie promise?"

She snorts. "You know I don't consider them binding, right?"

I hold up my hand between us, pinkie outstretched and say nothing.

She huffs. "Two pinkie promises in one day. A new record."

We hook fingers and shake.

"I'm honored that both belong to me. You do know that if you break a pinkie promise, I get to break the pinkie?"

"I'd like to see you try," she says and slips back inside the ship.

CHAPTER FIFTEEN

VANE

Darkland rises up from the horizon just after noon on the fourth day at sea.

Plumes of smoke curl in the sky like ghosts and that familiar scent of steel and ash immediately makes me feel at odds with myself. I made a life on Neverland, but Darkland will always be home. It doesn't mean I want to return to it.

Roc joins me at the railing as the harbor draws nearer.

"Needles," he states as the ship is steered toward Darkland's southwestern coast.

"Yep." I take a hit from my cigarette and hold the smoke in my lungs.

Needle Harbor sits on the edge of the Umbrage. I'm guessing Roc told the hired crew to sail there. The closer we are to our old neighborhood, the quicker we can retrieve the hat and leave.

Roc snaps his fingers at me and I hand him the cigarette. He takes a hit as we slip past the break wall and into Needles. At one point, Roc and I had a quarter share of the harbor. Nothing happened in these waters that we didn't know about.

To the left of the channel is the Bones Boardwalk, named after the Bone Society after its donation to the construction fund. The boardwalk curls around the jutting spot of land known as the Thumb where the black and white-stoned row houses are lined up like dominoes. We used to frequent the third house on the left, owned by an Umbrage boss best known for his ability to break legs.

Most of the people we ran with back then would be dead by now. They were mortals with mortal bones and mortal lives.

Roc hands the cigarette back now that it's nearly spent. I take the last hit and drop the butt in a bucket of water at my feet. The ember hisses out. I check my brother's profile looking for signs of his monster. So far he seems to be under control. But for how long? How long will my blood quell the chaos lurking beneath his skin?

"You still own the loft?" I ask him.

The ship sails past a smaller fishing boat. The man, pole in hand, turns to stare at us. Do these people know my name? So much has changed and yet everything is the same.

"I do." Roc props his forearms on the railing and leans over. "And the apartment above Lost Soul."

I raise a brow. "Really? And who owns Lost Soul?"

"One of Mog's descendants. Great-great whatever. He's a bit of a dick, but he liked getting fucked by me so I toler-ated him."

"And how do you think he'll feel now that you have a pirate and a queen on your arm?"

He pivots, leaning his hip into the ship's sidewall. "I don't *have* anyone."

"Oh? Could have fooled me."

"It's...still in flux."

"Is it?"

"I'm quite positive, baby brother, that I did not sign up to be analyzed."

I look over at him. He's smiling at me, feigning annoyance.

I missed him more than I realized.

For much of our early lives, we were inseparable. Roc was never the overprotective sort of brother. He believed in freedom and autonomy over anything else, but if I was ever in a bad spot, he was there. Always there. It's why Lainey's death was so hard for me to take. I always assumed if I couldn't protect her, Roc would. One of us would always be at her side.

Her death surprised me.

I thought we were invincible, making her invincible too. But she wasn't a monster like us. Our beast is inherited through the paternal line.

Maybe Lainey's death surprised Roc too. We've barely spoken of her.

We make it past the row houses, then the white clapboard house belonging to the seaguard. The channel widens into Needle Harbor where commercial ships dock on the right and leisure ships on the left. Dockhands are already waiting for us in an open slip at the front of the harbor.

"Will you make me a promise?"

I look back at Roc. "Depends."

"This is serious."

All the humor is gone from his face and his green eyes glint in the light.

"Okay."

"If I lose control in any way, you will kill me."

I'm angry at him in an instant. "Don't fucking say that."

"I will not descend into *madness*."

Madness. The word is multifaceted for us. The Madd brothers with a mother who leapt off a cliff, a father who tried to overthrow the monarchy, and an uncle who—

"Promise me."

"I don't have the blade," I say too quickly.

"It's in the loft."

"I'm not going to kill you."

He pushes away from the railing and straightens. He's exactly two inches taller than I am and he's never let me forget it. Now he's trying to use it to his advantage, to show his authority over me, his little brother. I've always wondered what is stronger: the shadow or the monster. Perhaps we will soon find out.

"I can't hurt them," he admits and his voice catches.

Hook and Wendy.

Apparently not so in flux after all.

The ship's crew calls out to one another, trimming the sails as we edge into the slip.

"It won't come to that," I tell him.

"But if it does?"

We've only ever seen one of our kind descend into madness, but we've never seen one get stuck in the monster, unable to turn back. But with the Myth Maker witch swirling around inside of him, anything is possible now.

He never should have devoured her. He knew better.

"Promise me," he says again.

If I were in his place, I know I'd be asking him the same. If I were on the verge of losing control, putting Winnie in danger, I'd beg him to kill me just like he is now.

"I'll promise under one condition."

"All right."

The crew tosses the mooring lines to the dockhands down below.

"We exhaust all options first. Including going *home* to look for our uncle."

He's the only one who's descended into madness and the only one I'd trust to know how to claw back.

Roc narrows his eyes at me. "Home, huh? You're not talking about Darkland."

"No."

"Well let's hope it doesn't come to that then."

"Let's hope."

The gangplank is hoisted down and secured to the wharf.

Roc holds out his hand to me and I reluctantly take it. We shake.

When I make a promise, I don't break it. But this one might be hard to swallow if it ever comes to paying it.

CHAPTER SIXTEEN

ROC

Darkland has been my home for so long that all of its flaws have blurred into the background. But now that I'm here with Wendy and the Captain, I can see it all.

The cobblestone streets are black-stained with soot. The buildings are crooked and stacked one on top of the other. Rainwater and the muck of a city is gathered in the gutters.

And yet, I feel immediately at home.

I love the Umbrage.

I love the grime and the people. I love the narrow streets laid out like a maze. So easy to get lost in. I love the hawkers and the newsboys and the grizzled fishermen.

But most of all, I love the outlaws.

They're everywhere in the Umbrage.

That boy on the next corner with the backwards news-cap, the tweed jacket, the toothpick in the corner of his mouth.

And the woman hurrying through the crowd pulling a child behind her. It's not her hands you have to watch, but the little girl's. They rush past an old man with a cane and the woman bumps into him, jostling the child. They apologize profusely. The man scowls.

The little girl gets a wallet for the trouble. The mom winks at her and they keep going.

In the Umbrage, anything is possible.

I'm at the head of our little ragtag group. Wendy is beside me, pretending she's not interested in my homeland even though she is. I can see her examining the streets and the people looking for things that remind her of me.

And the Captain on the other side of her in his long coat made of royal blue broadcloth, both pistols at his hips. He fits right in here.

Firecracker is nestled in one of the deep pockets of the Captain's coat, his paws curled over the edge. Honestly it didn't take much coaxing for the Captain to take in our kitten. He's already falling for the little beast.

Behind us, Vane, Winnie, and Asha. I don't have to see Asha to know she's taking in the details even more than Wendy is.

And Winnie Darling...she might be more of a feral cat than Firecracker.

"Take me to the place where you grew up," she's saying.

"Absolutely not," Vane replies.

"Why not?"

"We're here on a mission and the mission is not exhuming my past."

I look back over my shoulder. "Our childhood home is outside the city, Darling. It would take us a while to reach it and I suspect your boyfriend is in a hurry to leave."

Vane scowls at me. "Oh and you're so eager to see our childhood home?"

I turn back to the street. "I live there."

"What?" He comes around me and forces me to a full stop. "You live at the manor?"

"The Remaldis permitted me to buy it back. I've owned it for going on...well, *a long time*."

"Why didn't you tell me?"

I shrug like it's no big deal, but it is. I didn't tell him because I knew he'd react this way. He had his own life on Neverland. What I did with mine mattered not. And if I'm being totally honest, while the manor may be my primary residence on paper, I rarely step foot inside of it. The memories are too painful. The halls too quiet. The ghosts too plenty.

But the thought of someone else inhabiting it, that was something I could not bear, so I bought it.

"You should have told me," Vane says. The scowl is gone now, replaced by something that looks an awful lot like hurt.

"I'm telling you now."

He scoffs and returns to his Darling. But I know that won't be the last I hear of it.

We continue on. Vane said the hat was in the warehouse. We only have one warehouse. It's tucked at the end of a narrow alley just behind Vagaries and Wilcox on the northwest end of the Umbrage. On foot, we should be there within twenty minutes.

We walk in silence.

Finally, we come to Wilcox Avenue where Wilcox & Sons takes up the entire street corner, the front of it all in glass. Wilcox is known for their impeccable tailoring and imported suits. I own seven as of right now. When Vane and I ruled the Umbrage, we could walk into Wilcox any time of day or night and take what we wanted.

We cut down the alley where empty crates are stacked

up outside Wilcox, the bright green logo painted over the wooden slats.

"Do you remember exactly where the hat is?" I ask Vane as the alley spills into an unloading area that proceeds the warehouse bay door.

"The cabinet, if I had to guess," he says.

Next to the bay door is an unmarked man door with a giant padlock installed on a thick iron strap. The padlock is a combination, the wheels inside marked with the language of the Bone Society, the language of monsters.

I pick up the lock. The metal is cold in my hand, pitted with rust, but the wheels turn without complaint.

There are seven wheels, each with twenty-seven glyphs. I spin the dials, remembering the combination easily. Once it's inputted, I yank the wheelhouse down and the lock pops open.

"How long has it been since you were here?" Vane asks.

"Years, at least."

"Is the Variant collection still here?"

"Yes."

He turns to Winnie Darling. "Be careful what you touch."

"What is the Variant collection?" the Captain asks me.

"A collection of hats." I smile at him. He is not convinced.

Wendy looks slightly intrigued by all of this. Asha is practically salivating. She's heard of the Variant Collection. I can tell.

Winnie Darling grabs Vane's hand and squeezes.

I push the door in.

Diffused silver light spills in through the barred windows along the back wall. There are rows and rows of crates and trunks and stuffed shelves along the brick walls.

Dust swirls in the air.

I glance down at the floor and come to a stop.

There is a noticeable set of tracks in the layer of dust disappearing down an aisle of crates.

Should have known someone else would beat us here.

CHAPTER SEVENTEEN

ASHA

As soon as we're inside the warehouse, I know we're not alone. After all these years, I've honed the sixth sense of knowing when I'm being watched.

A man comes out of the farthest aisle of crates. I scan his face first, then his clothing. He's wearing a black wool jacket, no markings. There's the outline of a dagger strapped to his right forearm. He must be left-handed. No other weapons. No swords, no pistols.

His trousers are fitted, his black boots freshly polished. A flash of silver around his neck reveals a necklace, but the pendant at the end is tucked beneath his black button-up shirt.

There's a tattoo on his left ring finger—two interconnected Ms.

Myth Maker.

He has the olive complexion, tawny hair, and broad, aristocratic nose of the founding line of Makers—the del Coir family.

"Malachi," Roc says.

The man smiles. "It's been far too long, Crocodile."

I think over what I know about the Myth Makers. If I remember correctly, Malachi is third-rank Myth, so not on the Council, but if he has del Coir blood, he'll rule eventually, provided he can find his way back to Lostland.

The Myth Makers on the other isles like to pretend they are homeless, their island lost to the mists of the sea. But I don't buy that. I think they enchanted Lostland a long time ago so their enemies couldn't find it. They position themselves as vulnerable, without a place to belong, all while they plot and infiltrate. I didn't learn enough about the Makers until I'd left home, but sometimes I wonder if I returned to my palace if I would find a Maker's mark within the walls. My former husband couldn't have pulled off his coup without help.

"Please do tell me," Roc says, stepping forward, "why you have broken into my warehouse."

Malachi pushes away from the stack of crates and clasps his hands behind his back. He isn't as tall as Roc, but his shoulders are thicker, more muscle rippling beneath the taut lines of his jacket. Still, a Myth Maker isn't as powerful as whatever Roc is, so I'm not worried about a confrontation.

In general, I'm rarely worried about brawn. It's the intellect, the secrets that concern me.

"I heard you were busy in Everland." Malachi smiles.

I glance at Wendy and give her a quick nod, gesturing for her to step behind me and Roc, just in case.

I know she can hold her own, but depending on Malachi's intentions, Wendy could be a target and her powers are offensive, not defensive.

She sees my gesture and takes a step behind me.

"I'm always busy," Roc answers. "You know me, idle hands and all that."

"Yes. And Mareth?"

There it is. He already knows Roc devoured the witch.

"Let me ask you again." Roc takes another step. "Why have you broken into my warehouse?"

"I never knew you to be so impatient."

"I have an itch that I need to scratch and you are prohibiting me from scratching it."

"The hat."

A ripple of consternation rolls through us.

None of this is a coincidence.

All of the levity is gone from Roc's voice when he says, "Where is it?"

"Not here."

Darkness kicks up around Winnie and Vane. Vane tightens his hold on her.

I've never seen their shadow at work, but the way the hair is rising on the back of my neck, I'd say it's a force to be reckoned with.

"Now everyone calm down," Malachi says over Roc. "I have a proposition."

"I'm not in the deal-making mood," Roc answers.

Malachi shrugs. "I mean, you could kill me. But then you will never find the hat and really, what would be the point?"

Vane leans into Winnie and whispers, "Stay." Then he pulls away and steps around his brother, facing Malachi. Some of the darkness abates, but tendrils of it paint the diffused light. "What's the proposition?"

"Vane, you always were the logical one." He looks between the brothers. "I'm sure it will come as no surprise to you to hear that the Darkland monarchy is in disarray. The only surviving member of the Remaldi family is Juliette and right now, the Privy Council is trying to sell her off. But her claim to the throne is thin at best. There always were rumors she was a bastard. Not your type of bastard, of course." He winks at Roc. "As you can imagine, chaos is exactly what the Myth Makers feast on. They are in place to overthrow Darkland. I want to help you stop it."

Vane tsks. "You expect us to believe that?"

"I will not be without my own reward."

"Go on."

"Lostland being lost, obviously that's a lie. But it's not entirely without truth. The longer we're away from home, the fewer Myths on land, the harder it is to find it upon our return. If we spread ourselves too thin, it really will be lost. For good. They've become too fucking greedy, too sloppy. If you want to know my philosophy, I believe each island has a ruling class for a reason. Just like the Roman Empire in the mortal realm, the more you absorb, the more likely it is you will crumble."

He takes a breath and looks at Roc. "There's another Myth here named Amanon. One of the Seven. This Myth has a sister. I'm sure you've heard of her."

"Mareth," Roc guesses.

Malachi nods. "She knows you devoured her sister. She will come for you, here or Neverland or any of the other islands. So really, what choice do you have? It's better to partner with me."

Vane and Roc share a look. They say nothing to one another, but the silence stretches on, almost like their silence carries words.

Finally Vane says, "I assume you have a plan?"

"Of course." Malachi smiles. "I'm not sure if you heard, but after your role in the death of the Remaldi family, the Privy Council decided to requisition Maddred Manor."

Roc visibly tenses.

"They're hosting a ball there tonight to announce Juliette's engagement. It's to be her summer residence. That place is fucking frigid. It's the perfect place to escape the city's stinking heat. But I digress. The Myth will be there tonight. Kill her, and I'll give you the hat."

He extends his hand. "Do we have a deal?"

Regardless of whether or not Roc and Vane want to go through with this, I know they'll shake on it. I think Roc holds pinkie promises in higher regard than handshakes.

Both brothers shake.

"I'll see you tonight then," Malachi says. "It's black tie. Dress appropriately."

He breezes past us, the warehouse door slamming shut in his wake.

CHAPTER EIGHTEEN
WENDY

Once Malachi is gone, Roc and Vane lead us to their loft with no discussion about the latest turn of events. Just a few blocks to the north of the warehouse, it doesn't take us long to reach it. The stairway is tucked to the right of a tavern entrance, with a hat shop on the other side. Coincidence or not? I'm beginning to wonder about the hat connections to Roc and Vane's family.

First, a magical hat that can remove Mareth's soul, then a collection of hats so dangerous, we're warned not to touch them?

I noticed Asha's interest at the mention of the Variant Collection. She always knows more than most.

Roc flips a light switch and one by one, hanging globes ignite with gas, then light.

I look around.

This is the first real thing of Roc's I've been immersed in. Being with him or around him, everything I encountered was limited or controlled.

There is nowhere to hide here, but glancing at him, he

doesn't seem to be affected by it. There is no air of vulnerability to him.

The loft is mostly one big, connected space, with a kitchen on the right of the entrance and a living space to the left with a table at the far end of the room set beneath a bank of cloudy windows twice as high as Roc is tall. Any daylight allowed to spill through the windows has a green cast to it. Most of the Umbrage is like this, dark and gritty and sallow. Roc seems right at home here.

He goes to the kitchen and pulls out several glasses with one hand, setting them on the long island that separates the kitchen from the living space. As he pours a round of drinks, I wander the perimeter of the room.

There are two additional doors branching off from the main loft. Peeking into the first one, I find a bathroom with black stone floors and a copper clawfoot tub. The second door leads to a large bedroom. There's a king-sized bed with a headboard made of black metal spindles. The bedding—black and silky—is pulled taut as if the bed were made and measured at the end of a ruler.

I keep wandering. Books are stacked up on a few end tables, some on the stone window ledges. Classic monster stories, mythologies, history of the Isles, and the mortal realm.

There's a thick stone ashtray on a coffee table with just a dusting of ash inside.

Roc offers everyone a drink, and when he comes to me, he holds the glass back, a questioning glint in his eyes. "Are you seeing anything of interest, Your Majesty?"

I let my attention wander away from him. There's an oil painting on the wall beside the bedroom door. There's a queen in the distance, standing on a moor, but she's pale, grotesque, and it looks like she's screaming. The sky is stormy and bruised. In the foreground, a dark shadow with pale green eyes.

"Who are you? Really?"

He finally gives me the glass. He takes a sip from his. He doesn't take his eyes off me, but I can't tell if he's looking out or inviting me in, all the way to the dark center of who he is.

"Who am I?" He smirks at me. "Who are you, Wendy Darling?"

There is a challenge in his words. Not to define either of us. But to reject the notion that we must be defined.

It reminds me of a poem Asha read me once, the original text smuggled into the Seven Isles from the mortal realms.

Do I contradict myself?

Very well then I contradict myself,

(I am large, I contain multitudes.)

Roc is many things: man and monster and dark, tempting myth. Perhaps in my desire to know him for who he really is, I fooled myself into believing he could be known. Can any of us be known? Truly for who we are?

I glance over the rise of Roc's shoulder at James. He's staring at us both, watching, waiting. If Roc is the gale force always propelling us forward, then James is the life raft, making sure we don't drown.

I need both of these men in different ways, but I don't think I can truly be with anyone until I figure out who I am, multitudes in all.

All of the years I fought to survive in the Everland court, I kept telling myself that once I escaped it, I would finally be allowed to live the life I wanted. Mine was stolen from me so early on, first by Peter Pan, then by King Hald.

Maybe somewhere along the way, I started to believe

my life was never going to be my own. And that belief has swallowed me up slowly, year after year, like a dark stain.

"This is a trap, you know," Vane says.

I blink, look away from James and back to Roc.

"Drink your drink, Your Majesty," he tells me and then pulls away, breaking the tension between us.

I almost stumble forward as if his attention was a crutch I needed to keep myself upright.

I bring the glass to my lips and pull in a sip. The liquor is a welcomed bite.

"Of course it's a trap." Roc goes around to the kitchen and leans his backside against the counter. He lights a cigarette and the smoke curls up into the high ceiling, spinning around the hanging globe lights. "The question is, who is setting it? Malachi crossing us is too obvious and he would know that. I think he wants what he says he wants. The question is, is he being discreet about it all?"

"What's your witch saying?" Asha asks. She's pulled herself up on the island, her legs dangling over the edge.

Roc sets his glass aside. "She is against working with him."

"That could also be a trap," Vane says.

Roc snorts. "Is everything a trap to you?"

"Yes," Winnie answers with a laugh. "He is suspicious of everyone."

"That's because everyone is suspicious."

Asha hops off the island. "Do you think it's a coincidence that they've seized your manor house?"

This is the elephant in the room, surely. I've been thinking about it ever since Malachi mentioned it.

"A coincidence?" Roc asks. "No. It was a targeted decision. There are at least a hundred mansions and manors on Darkland. It didn't have to be that one."

"What is their reason for wanting that one, then?" Asha asks, but I know her well. She's not asking because she needs an answer, she's asking because she already knows and she needs it confirmed.

"Here's the plan." Vane breaks away from Winnie and comes to the center of the room. It's hard not to be instantly drawn to him. Much like Roc, there's something magnetic about Vane. I used to think it was their good looks, which yes, is likely some of it. But now I wonder if it's also their power, the monster that lurks beneath. It must give them a certain kind of presence that is impossible to ignore.

"You are staying here." Vane points at Roc. "And both of you should stay with him." He nods at me and James next. "Both of you are a weakness for him and whatever is going on here, he is the center."

I don't want to admit it, but hearing Vane acknowledge my importance to Roc makes my stomach ignite with butterflies. No one knows Roc better than Vane. And yes, Roc did *reassure me* on the ship, but there's something about a third-party confirmation that just makes it more real.

"Asha and I will go to the manor."

"And me?" Winnie crosses her arms over her chest anticipating a fight.

"You'll stay here."

She tilts her head and gives him a look, popping out a hip while she does.

"Win," he says, almost a growl.

"The shadow is more powerful when it's together. Exiling me here only inhibits it."

"She has a point," Roc says.

"Shut up. You don't know anything about the shadow."

"I mean, half plus half equals one. I do know how to count."

"Fine." Vane spreads out his arms, a show of deference. At this point, I don't know why he tries to fight her. She clearly, always, wins.

"You, Asha and I will go to the manor," he goes on. "I will kill the Myth to fulfill our obligation to Malachi and as soon as he's given us the hat, I will kill him too."

"Now, there's no need to get passive-aggressive about it." Roc bends down to scoop up Firecracker and cradles the cat in his arms. "Malachi is doing what you or I would have done if we needed to keep our hands clean."

"I don't care. I'm still killing him."

Firecracker digs his claws into Roc's shirt and climbs up on his shoulder. "I feel it's my duty to point out that by killing Malachi, we surrender a potential ally in this fight against the Myths. Mareth, her sister, Amanon, I can guarantee they aren't the only ones on Lostland plotting the occupation of the Seven Isles."

Vane crosses his arms over his chest. "He broke into the warehouse."

"Yes, and he could have taken anything. He took a hat."

"This time. What will he take the next?"

"Don't kill him," Roc finally says, and there is a finality in his voice.

Vane grumbles but doesn't further the argument.

"Now that that's settled, let's talk about attire." Roc reaches up to scratch Firecracker beneath the chin and the cat leans into the attention. "My closet may have a suit for you, but I'm short a few ball gowns for the ladies."

"Is Lia's shop still around?" Vane asks.

"Yes. Same building. Different owner."

"I'll take them." He starts for the door.

"Can I come?"

Vane stops, hand on the door handle. He looks back at me, considering the request before checking his brother for permission. Roc shrugs. "I don't own her."

"I wouldn't mind spending more time with Winnie while we have it," I say.

I may have been queen of an entire kingdom, but I still had to ask for permission for literally anything I wanted to do. The habit is still trailing me like a ghost.

Winnie comes over, threading her arm around my shoulders. "I'd love that."

I warm beneath her touch. The way she so easily shows affection is something I admire and yet don't understand. Touching was prohibited in court. It was seen as obscene, unseemly. Touching only happened behind closed doors, preferably in the dark. Being touched, needing to feel skin-to-skin contact, it wasn't something any of us were encouraged to admit.

"We'll make a date of it." Winnie smiles over at me.

"We'll all go then." Roc snaps his fingers at James. "You're coming too."

"I don't want to go dress shopping."

"Too bad."

James grumbles but follows the order. On his ship, he may be used to being in charge, but when it comes to Roc, he and I have both met our match.

THE FRONT OF LIA'S SHOP REMINDS ME OF STRIPED CANDIES. THE columns are painted bright green while the facade is painted soft, salmon pink. The delicate hand-carved cornices are gilded in gold.

The recessed entrance is flanked by two bay windows where several wooden mannequins display a collection of fine dresses, some ballgowns, others day dresses.

Roc pushes the door in, jangling the copper bell that hangs above. He holds the door for our entire party to shuffle in.

Soft light flickers in hanging globe pendants, not too dissimilar to the lighting in Roc's loft.

Over the years, on Everland, I had a general feeling that we were behind in advancements. People visited our courts from other islands and while they would never come right out and say it, I got the sense they were missing luxuries from their homelands.

Most of our lighting was candle or kerosene. It wasn't until the last handful of years that some of the merchants along the waterline had started pushing the privy council to install modern lighting. Of course, the council liked to keep us in the dark ages, literally. The merchants hadn't managed to gain much progress.

The lighting that I've seen here on Darkland seems to be some kind of gas. The globes dance with light, like flame trapped in a bottle. It's mesmerizing.

"Do my eyes deceive me?" a voice calls from the back of the shop. "Has the Crocodile decided to grace my shop once again?"

"Oh, don't badger me, Antony," Roc says. "I'm here now."

A man, half as tall as Roc, comes flitting out of the dress racks. He's wearing a black suit with a bow tie the same salmon pink as the storefront. His hair is bleached nearly white, his beard too, so that it stands out starkly against his dark skin.

Several green stones wink from silver settings in his ears.

"Badgering you is my favorite hobby." Antony comes to a stop at Roc's side. "You've..." He narrows his eyes and looks him up and down. "Changed? What's different about you?"

"A great many things," is what Roc says.

"I'll say." Antony reaches out, hooking his arm through Roc's, cozying up to him.

James takes a step, pushing his hook between Roc and Antony.

Both men glance at James and I see the sudden surprise dawn on James's face.

"I...*he*..." James crumbles. "Please get your hands off him."

Antony cocks his head back. "Oh. Okay. Okay." He looks up at Roc. "Someone's finally managed to snag you?"

"When a handsome pirate claims me, who am I to resist?"

Antony chuckles. It's the kind of deep, rich laughter that makes everything feel lighter and airier.

"It's not like that," James says.

Antony squeezes James's hand as he moves away. "It doesn't have to be anything, friend. Just let it be what it is."

Roc swings his arm around James and pulls him down the aisle, following in Antony's footsteps. "Yes, Captain. Just let us be what we are."

I sense the air shifting beside me. "You know you can claim him too?" Winnie whispers.

Asha and Vane disappear into the clothing racks, pretending to look at the clothing while secretly plotting the strategy. They've only met, but Asha seems right at home with Roc and Vane. As if they understand one another.

We wander down an aisle, then around a rack of simple cotton dresses. Roc and James come into view again. Roc is so tall that he's easy to spot across the racks of clothing.

There is agency in claiming something, in deciding it belongs to you. But nothing has ever belonged to me. Peter Pan kidnapped me when I was eighteen and I never returned home. Not even my own baby, my own flesh and blood, belonged to me. She was taken from my arms, smuggled a world away.

Everything I've ever had, has been stolen from me.

Everything I had in the Everland Court, I knew, deep down, belonged to Hald and that he could rip it away again at any moment.

"I'm afraid." The words slip out of me without thinking about what they might cost.

Winnie tilts her head, regarding me like a puzzle piece, defining my edges as if to decide where I might fit best.

"Why?" she asks.

"They abandoned me once. They can again." My vision goes watery with tears. "And now they have this entire thing without me. I don't want to ruin their equilibrium."

Winnie snorts. "Have you ever thought to ask yourself if you *are* the equilibrium?"

I frown. "What do you mean?"

"If there is anything I've learned about being with Vane and Pan, Bash and Kas—"

"Wait, you're with all four of them?" My question comes out almost a wheeze of incredulity.

"Yes? You didn't know?"

"I think I thought it was Vane and Pan, mostly. The twins...I guess I wasn't sure."

"The twins aren't as obvious about it as Vane and Pan. Kas and Bash aren't as possessive or territorial. But yes, I'm with all four of them. We've negotiated all of the pitfalls of a five-person relationship. And trust me, there are a lot. But what I was saying is, while I might have come to them very late in their relationships, and I could have easily felt like a fifth wheel, I quickly learned they needed me just as much as I needed them. Hook and Roc might have established something before finding you—which honestly, the fact I'm even saying that is wild, trust me, they were trying to kill each other not that long ago. But anyway, what I mean is, you are not a third wheel. They need you for who you are, just like you need them for who they are. You just have to figure out what that is and embrace it."

We pass a rack of hairbands that are sequined and embroidered and feathered. "You are my great-great-great something granddaughter, and somehow, I feel like you are far wiser than I ever was."

She chuckles and takes my hand affectionately. "There's this saying in my world—our world—fake it till you make it. I'm mostly just faking it."

We laugh together.

"What is our world like now? What is something you think might surprise me?"

"Hmmm, oh god. Let me think. There's so much." We keep walking the perimeter of the store. "Oh here's a good one. Women can finally own property."

I pull away. "Truly?"

She nods. "And bank accounts."

We make it to the back of the shop. Vane and Asha have decided on a green dress for Winnie, and while I took Winnie for a person who likes to be in charge of her own destiny, she gives no resistance, proving that perhaps she is the most measured woman I've ever met.

I like her more and more every minute.

Asha decides on a billowy black dress—"To hide my weapons"—and Vane picks out a tux.

While they finalize the sales, I admire a gorgeous red dress on a mannequin nestled in an arched alcove. The bodice is formfitting with hundreds of sequins sewn into it. The skirt is layers and layers of tulle, but there's a slit just off center to show off the wearer's thigh.

"This one too," I hear Roc say behind me.

"That's an excellent selection." Antony sidles up near me. "With your complexion, and dark hair, it'll look fabulous on you."

"Oh. No. I mean, I don't have any money and this must cost a fortune." I meet Roc's gaze. He's not looking at the dress, but directly at me, when he says, "Take it off the floor, Antony. Charge it to my tab."

Antony winks at me. "Right away."

A few workers appear from the back and all of our purchases are folded and backed into tissue, then into boxes.

"You didn't have to do that," I say to Roc. "I have no occasion to wear it. It's a waste of your money."

"Oh I didn't buy it for you," he answers.

"I'm confused."

"It was mostly self-serving. I wanted the opportunity to rip it from your body sometime in the near future." He winks at me.

A blush burns through my cheeks.

"And that, Your Majesty, is exactly why I bought that dress. Impropriety makes you flush and I find it fucking hot. I will have you begging for depravity before long."

Antony calls him away, leaving me blinking at the now naked mannequin, face burning, liquid heat pooling between my legs.

CHAPTER NINETEEN

ROC

The blood is wearing off faster and faster.

He watches them discuss the plan.

He watches them slip into the clothing. The dresses. The tux.

He lights a cigarette to take the edge off. Downs a shot of expensive rum. Then another. He can't sit still. If he sits still, he slips.

He needs more of Vane's blood, but he can't keep chugging it back. Where they're from, there is a cost to everything and eventually there will be a cost to this too.

The light at the end of the tunnel fades.

Don't worry, the witch says. *I'll take care of you.*

He can hear Wendy's voice, the rising lilt of it.

It reminds him of wind rushing through leaves.

A lull.

A lull.

The light is just a pinprick now, the world muffled around him.

The cigarette is burning down to the end, caught between his knuckles.

Go on, the witch says. *I'll take care of you. Just let me—*

♩

"Drink."

I blink up at my brother.

Vane is lined in the silver moonlight pouring through the loft windows. He's in the tux, his hair combed over.

The witch's voice goes silent. She doesn't like Vane. He's a man that is hard to like.

The moonlight catches the blood in the bottom of a shot glass held firmly in Vane's grip.

"We're almost there," he says. "Go on."

What choice do I have? They're leaving me alone with the Captain and Wendy. If I can't keep it together—

I take the glass and swig it back.

"You were beginning to shift again," he tells me and when I look past him to the others, I can see their apprehension, confirming it.

"It's not lasting as long, is it?" he asks. Not really a question.

"We're almost there," I say, echoing him, and he nods.

"I'll take care of the Myth. It won't be hard. I'll get the hat and you will be well."

"I know." The words don't sound confident though and Vane catches on.

"Do you have the blade?" I ask him and he winces. "It's in the bedroom in the place where we leave our blades."

"It hasn't come to that."

"Hasn't it?"

"I'm not willing to risk the blade, not at the manor. It stays here."

He has a good point.

"We're ready." Asha's at the door. The dress she selected is just a different version of her soldier's uniform—material dark as night, so easy to hide in shadows. Material made to move so she can fight her way out of a tight spot.

Between Vane, Winnie, and Asha, I almost pity the Myth.

"Thank you for doing this." I set the glass aside, the bottom still coated thick with red.

Vane nods. "Thank me once I bring you the hat. And do not leave. Promise me."

"Pinkie promise." I hold out my little finger for him. He snorts and turns away.

Firecracker jumps in my lap and turns a circle, then kneads at my thigh. The little devil digs his claws into my flesh, but the pain helps drive away some of the fuzziness still permeating my awareness.

The witch may have been driven back by the new dose of blood, but she's no longer quiet. I should be worried. I *am* worried.

"We won't be long."

And then they're gone.

CHAPTER TWENTY
VANE

WE'VE RENTED A CARRIAGE TO TAKE US TO THE MANOR. IT'S A thing of luxury, with the twin bench seats upholstered in red velvet and the walls in black leather. Two small lanterns flicker from the outside casting soft light through the windows.

It may be a luxury, but when your standard mode of transportation is flying, everything pales in comparison.

I fidget in my seat.

Winnie takes my hand in hers, fingers threaded together.

The shadow sighs with contentment.

When we are apart, it riots.

When we are together, it calms.

When we are skin on skin, it settles into our hollows like a tide filling up a million tiny pools.

I almost sigh with it.

"Historically, shadows have never been split," Asha says from the bench across from us. "How did you manage it?"

"Shadows do what shadows want," is my answer, at the

same time Winnie says, "It claimed me and when Vane was pushed off a cliff, I begged it to claim Vane too."

"She's downplaying it, of course," I add. "She leapt off the cliff after me. The woman who is afraid of heights."

"*Recovering* from a fear of heights." She smiles. "You gain the ability to fly, and gravity is no longer a burden."

Asha's gaze cuts between us. "You Maddred brothers like strong women."

A statement. A fact. An observation.

If you had asked me this time last year, I would have denied it. The Darkland Dark Shadow liked to terrify. It wanted to chase and fuck and dominate. It needed to feel superior. There were days when even being around Pan was difficult because the shadow knew he was more powerful than it.

Some of that could have been attributed to the fact that the shadow and I were never a compatible match and it hated being off its island. The Neverland Shadow is different in every way. Agreeing to split itself being one of them. And I never get the feeling the Neverland Shadow is just one bad day away from tearing me apart from the inside out.

The carriage clatters to a halt at a busy intersection. We're out of the Umbrage now and into the Merchant Quarter on the outskirts of Dark City. Darkland is made up of several mid-sized cities, with Dark City being its biggest. Everything else revolves around it, almost like a sundial. Even the Umbrage for all of its misfit, rebellious ways. Maddred Manor is on the northwest end of Dark City, halfway between the city and Port Night on the island's northern coast.

When traffic is clear, we lurch forward straight through the intersection and through the Quarter.

Winnie is hunched forward trying to get the best view out the window. Darkland and Neverland couldn't be more different from one another. Neverland is wilder, with a certain element of freedom. Darkland was always about restriction and control. I hated everything about it. And I didn't realize just how much until our father was exiled, our titles stripped away. I struggled for so long with the Darkland Dark Shadow because it wanted to return and I did not. But giving it up... I was always acutely aware that giving it away meant giving its power to someone else and that was never an option. I think deep down, I always knew it had to be Roc. I wouldn't trust the shadow with anyone else.

We pass a few shops that were once swarming with activity last I was here and are now boarded up, windows smashed, front facades scarred and stained.

It takes me by surprise, and it must show because Asha says, "There was a riot here years back. Fighting between the ruling class and the poor."

"Roc didn't tell me."

"Probably because it never affected him. He could easily stand with the poor and turn around and party with the wealthy. They both loved him."

"Was it settled then? The fighting? I'm surprised they haven't rehabilitated the buildings."

"The poor were driven back," Asha explains. "Then double-taxed the year after. I think the ruin is meant to remind them of what happens when they get out of line."

The wealthy and noble in Darkland always did embrace the lie that they were better than the lower class. Noble born meant superior blood. And while the merchant class could never fully penetrate the nobility, they were happy to be in close proximity to it, sure that when the time came, they would be protected from whatever ills plagued the lower class.

With the Merchant Quarter behind us, the large brownstones start to dominate the streets. Most of these houses belong to wealthy merchants, and most of them are designed by Hil Howe, a semi-famous architect from the mortal realm. He's dead now, which has only added to the value of the houses.

"How far now?" Winnie asks.

I glance out the window to get my bearings. A three-story neoclassical comes into view. The front facade is constructed of white limestone, the columns ornate, the windows rounded with decorative white stone hoods. If I remember correctly, it belongs to a textile merchant known as the Silk Baron.

"We're close," Asha answers before I can.

"You know Darkland well."

"I do."

"How long did you live here?"

"Many years."

"For someone known for their precision, that's an awfully un-precise answer."

She just stares at me.

In her dress, hair pinned back, she could be any noble-woman. Clothing elegant and fashionable, but eyes a little vacant, either out of boredom or disinterest. How quickly she can disappear into a role. How dangerous she must be.

"What's your favorite part of Darkland?" Winnie asks.

She's always been hungry for crumbs of my life before Neverland. As if knowing my past will peel back the layers of who I am in the present.

If only she knew how much of myself I abandoned in

order to have my revenge and survivor it. If only she knew how much Peter Pan changed me.

Asha considers the question carefully. "The Night Gardens."

"The name alone," Winnie says.

"Yep." Asha watches a man walk past on the sidewalk as we wait for another break in traffic. "All of the foliage is either black or white. And under a full moon, the white flowers almost glow. It's absolutely beautiful."

Winnie glances at me. "Do you know it?"

"Of course."

"Can we go to it?"

"If we have time in between murder and blackmail, sure."

Asha laughs. "I know that was a joke, but I can tell murder and blackmail are also not out of the ordinary for you."

I wish that wasn't the case.

I wish a great many things.

The carriage finally breaks through the traffic and we cross the next intersection and there, at the end of the street, the large, wrought iron gate proceeding the long, winding drive to Maddred Manor on the rise of a gently sloping hillside.

Maddred, much like its name and the family origin, is constructed in bright, blood-red stone. Its main structure in the center of the manor is three stories, with a balcony on the second and third floors. It's bounded on both sides by east and west wings with only two stories. Unlike the neoclassical brownstones outside the Merchant Quarter, the manor's architectural style is hard to label here in the Seven Isles because its style did not originate here.

The size of it may be grand, but the style is minimalistic, almost military-like in its sharpness and its unadornment. My father wanted it that way. My mother wanted the soft, country style of the northern coast houses. It was her money, but it was our father who always got the last word.

The horses come to a stop as the carriage driver announces our name. The gate quickly swings inward, permitting our entrance.

I didn't think coming here would affect me. But I'm suddenly feeling affected.

The shadow surges to me, its energy flooding my veins with a calming antidote.

My hand still in hers, Winnie hooks her other arm around my elbow, pulling me even closer.

I'm all right, is what I want to say, but she would know it's a fucking lie.

The shadow hides nothing.

A half-dozen carriages are already lined up, waiting for their occupants to depart at the portico as we clatter up the drive.

"Let's go over the plan one more time," I say.

"We stay together until we identify the witch," Winnie says.

"Then we separate," Asha adds. "And stand as backup."

"Once I've completed the task, you find Malachi to confirm. If he doesn't have the hat on him, I will yank his insides out his fucking nose."

"No, you won't." Winnie pats my thigh. "Because once he's dead, we won't know where he put this magical hat."

"Then I'll force the hat's location out of him and then yank his insides out his fucking nose."

Winnie gives me a look. It's not a threatening look. There is nothing menacing about it. It's just cold and distant and detached, like she's inside her own head plotting all the ways she will torture me until I beg for forgiveness.

And for her, torture isn't blood and gore and guts. It's psychological warfare.

"Do you want to go over the actual dispensing of a Myth?" Asha asks. "They aren't easy to—"

"*Kill*. Yes, I know. But I have the dark shadow. And what better way to fight darkness than with something darker?"

"So you plan to kill her how? You never did tell me."

"The shadow moves between us," Winnie explains. "So I'll push it toward Vane."

"And at full power, the shadow can tear arms from bodies, muscle from bone. It will be messy, but thankfully not my mess to clean up. I'll leave that to Malachi."

"How will you get her somewhere private?"

This is the part I hate the most and explaining it is akin to ripping out my own insides through my nose.

Winnie lowers her voice and leans across the carriage like she's about to share a secret. "I'm not sure if you noticed, but women have a hard time ignoring Vane."

"So you're going to seduce her?" Asha's voice rises with incredulity.

"I have a less than ten percent fail rate," I reassure her.

"You don't think the Myth will see you and immediately be suspicious?"

"What are the myths well known for?"

"Manipulation. Persuasion. Compliance."

"Yes, and their hubris is often their undoing. She may be suspicious of me, but there is an opportunity to exploit it, because the suspicion is also a challenge to bend me to her will. She won't, of course. I cannot be persuaded."

"Hah!" Winnie shouts. "I can persuade you to do a great many things."

"I don't need to know," Asha says.

The carriage pulls forward again. We're next in line to disembark.

"To pull it off, of course, I need to keep my hands to myself," Winnie says. "It will be the most difficult task, but I'm willing to power through it." She smiles innocently at me.

That look, the brattiness...fuck, if we were alone right now...

She senses my shift in thought and winks at me, knowing full well where my attention has gone.

Finally, we're beneath the portico. One of the servants pulls the carriage door open, setting a stool beneath. I get out first so I can offer my hand to Winnie, then Asha.

The girls right themselves, smoothing over their dresses.

I walk forward to the bottom of the steps and look up.

Wind rattles the leaves of the oak trees.

Blood is pumping through my veins, but I feel hollow.

I'm not an anxious person, but sometimes a feeling like anxiety will creep up and whenever it does, I revert to something I've read, repeating it in my head like a mantra.

More often than not, it's Poe. I read him often. For some reason, his poetry helps me make sense of the darkness, the monstrous things, the abyss at the center of me, threatening to swallow me whole.

Being here at the manor again, I can't help but think of all of the loss. All of the fucking ghosts.

The spirits of the dead, who stood,
In life before thee, are again,
In death around thee, and their will,
Shall overshadow thee; be still.

I didn't want to return here.

Winnie comes up beside me. "I'm here," she whispers.

"I know."

"I love you."

"I love you too."

"Now let's go kill some witches, and then afterward, I'll shove you down in my bed and have my way with you."

When I look over at her, she's beaming at me and I huff out a laugh.

CHAPTER TWENTY-ONE

ROC

He is transfixed by the sight of Captain James Hook lighting a cigarillo, lips wrapping around the end of it, lungs drawing in the hit.

"What is it?" the Captain asks, frowning across the room at him.

Wendy pours them all a drink. She's chattering on about its recipe, a staple of the Everland Court. Something with rose syrup and gin and lemon juice. She's busying herself with the task, measuring out each ingredient with the precision of a scientist.

She is nervous to be alone with them again. The first time since they fucked in the Everland Palace.

He is ravenous for them both.

The witch spins beneath the surface like a whirlpool threatening to pull him down.

The Captain tests the gin straight from the bottom and grimaces. "Awful," he says.

"The rose syrup tempers the gin," Wendy is saying. "Wait to try the drink before you dismiss it."

"Very well."

She opens a drawer, then another. "Where are your spoons?"

She's looking at us.

Speak.

Say something.

"Roc?"

"Second drawer from the left."

He wants to throw Wendy on the counter and eat her pussy until she cries. He wants to bend the Captain over the couch and fuck him until he can't see straight.

And then we will devour them.

He snaps to.

No.

Yes.

"Roc?"

THE GLASS IN WENDY'S OUTSTRETCHED HAND IS FILLED WITH bright candy pink liquid. "Are you okay?"

I'm hard and hungry and horrified.

"I can't stay here." I lurch out of the chair.

"What?" She sets the glass on the nearest table.

The Captain cuts me off. "What's wrong?"

I pull in a deep breath and slam my eyes shut. If I look at him too long, too closely, I will fall deeper and deeper and I don't know if I can climb my way out.

You do not control me.

If you say so, the witch answers.

"I need more blood. I need Vane's blood." I step around him for the door.

"Right now?"

"Yes. Now."

"He made you promise not to leave," Wendy says.

"He didn't pinkie promise."

Wendy snorts. The Captain crosses the room to me and puts his hook above the door handle. "If you insist on going, we're going with you."

I glance at them over my shoulder. Wendy, smaller on the other side of the room, looking pale and helpless. The Captain beside me, bigger, but somehow more fragile.

"You will be at risk."

"So?" the Captain says.

"So. I won't have it."

Wendy rushes forward and wraps her hand around my wrist. "You don't get to tell us when and how we show up for you."

This is exactly what the witch wants, is what I think. But I can't say that. I can't look weak. I can't look like I care so much it hurts.

"If you insist."

"Give us ten minutes." Wendy turns back for the bedroom where her new dress is hanging in the closet. "And then we'll go. James, can you summon a carriage?"

"Of course." To me, he says, "Sit down. Smoke a cigarette. Have a drink."

I close my eyes again. "Yes, Captain."

He sighs. It comes out through his nose. It makes my insides light up.

Before them, I had one vulnerability: Vane. But he's nearly invincible. Wendy and the Captain...they are not as impervious. Strong, but not without weakness.

And the thing that poses them the most danger?

It might be me.

With the Captain out hailing a cab, and Wendy now in the bathroom readying herself, I slip into my bedroom.

There's a lamp on the bedside table. I unscrew the bolt at the top and pop off the cloth shade. The outer workings come off with another pop and what remains is the hilt of a blade.

A hidden button on the back of the lamp's base releases the blade, and the weapon slides free.

It's about half the length of my forearm, made of a specific kind of metal that does not exist here. The handle is thornewood, weathered now by age and use.

I can recall my uncle's words when he gave me the blade all those years ago.

Swift and keen, and always ready for service.

Upon first glance, it would be easy to mistake the blade for nothing more than a kitchen knife.

Maybe it was always meant to be overlooked.

Because this blade, in particular, is the only type of blade that can kill Vane and me. The only one capable of killing monsters. *Our monsters.*

I slide the knife into a sheath strapped to my left forearm and hide it beneath my shirt sleeve.

CHAPTER TWENTY-TWO

ASHA

There is such a thing as too much information, and right now, I'm nearing overload.

There is symbolism in everything in Darkland. From the Statue of the Dark in the city center meant to symbolize the liberation that comes with embracing the dark. To the serpents often carved or painted or molded into building edifices, declaring their natural inclination to protect and defend what is theirs. To the skulls stamped into their coinage, symbolizing death and rebirth.

Maddred Manor is no different. It lacks any of the ornate architecture common amongst the nobility. Showing strength in restraint, which is ironic considering the manor was seized from the family due to the patriarch's greed.

I trail behind Vane and Winnie as they make their way up the stairs—three separate tiers with steps that curve outward like a crescent moon.

When we reach the grand front entrance, lighted by an oversized caged lantern, I come to a sudden stop.

There is a coat of arms carved into the stone above the double doors.

My theory, realized.

I know that crest.

As is traditional for Darkland coat of arms, there's a knight's helm at the top, one of the medieval kind with a slit for the eyes, and a giant black plume rising from the crown. Behind the helm is a red and black flourish. Beneath is the shield with the crescent moon and two stars, flanked by the standard two supporting figures: a raven and a skeleton.

The family motto is beneath in old darkish: *viere magnar, mori melius.*

Live great, die better.

The presence of the coat of arms confirms my earlier suspicions.

Winnie catches my hesitation. "You coming?"

Vane follows my line of sight and scowls when he sees what I see.

"Should we be worried?" I ask.

Vane's scowl deepens. "About what?"

"Yeah." Winnie glances between us. "About what?"

"That family crest," I say, more to her than to Vane, because he clearly knows what it means. "It belongs to the Corbeld family. The matriarchal line of Vane and Roc's family."

"Your mother?" Winnie echoes and the way Vane tenses up tells us all we need to know.

"And after the Lorne family, the Corbelds were next in line for the throne. Making Roc—"

Vane is swift, grabbing Winnie first, then me, ushering us into the shadows of the bushes that line the front of the house. "We were stripped of our titles," he says quickly.

"Maybe at one point, Roc was fifth in line for the throne, but he is no longer. Our father's actions made sure of that."

Winnie crosses her arms over her chest, listening intently.

"It was the Lorne family that took your standing from you and the Lornes are no longer in charge. Do you think the Myths couldn't make a case for Roc if that was what they wanted?"

Vane grumbles, but the sound hums between his teeth.

Winnie catches on quickly because she's smart and not clouded by eons of family baggage. At least not when it comes to the Maddred family.

"You think the Myths are trying to install Roc on the Darkland throne?" she asks.

"Yes," is my answer.

"They would need to control him…"

"Yes," I say. "Ask Vane if that's possible. If when you devour something powerful enough, it can hijack your body."

"It's unprecedented," he says quickly.

"But not impossible?" Winnie asks.

He finally breaks his scowl. "Not impossible."

"That's why you've pulled away from me." Winnie steps in front of him, forcing him to look down at her. "I thought it was because you were focusing on the mission. I thought you were pulling the shadow to you and because of it, the connection between us weakened. But no, you're purposefully keeping me out because you're afraid."

"I am not afraid."

"Then open the connection."

I wait, unsure of how this connection works and whether or not I'll know once it's open. It's fascinating watching them communicate and interact with the shadow. They seem to have an almost telepathic connection. I'm not interested so much in science, or the study of the supernatural in the Seven Isles, but the archivist in me is curious about any overlap in the well-documented history of the Isles. A connection like this could not only be a weakness but an incredible strength. It explains why Neverland's standing in the Isles is slowly gaining ground again. Pan has always been a prominent figure, but some of his influence waned when he lost his shadow. Now that they have both Neverland shadows, they've defeated Hook and the Fae Queen, the rest of the Isles are going to think twice about crossing Pan.

I'm getting off track.

Focus, Ash.

Winnie huffs out of frustration, so I can only assume Vane has not opened the connection.

"We complete this mission," she says, "we get the hat from Malachi, and then all of this will be moot. Or at least the part where the Myths try to possess Roc and use him to overthrow the Darkland monarchy. I guess whether or not Roc wants to be King of Darkland is up to him."

"He never wanted to rule," Vane admits.

"Roc loves being pampered," Winnie says.

"Irrelevant. Being fifth in line, you're never intended to rule. He embraced all of the trappings of royalty and was allowed to ignore the duty. I'm not sure where he'd land now, but he's never been one for *responsibility*."

"Okay, you have a point." Winnie takes a breath. "The good thing is, Roc has promised to stay home, out of harm's way."

Vane glances over at her. "Yes, but do you trust him to keep that promise?"

"Well, I'm sure...I mean...*maybe*..."

Vane grumbles again and then starts for the door. "Let's get this over with. The sooner I kill this Myth, the sooner we can be free of this nightmare."

We're ushered in through the foyer by staff dressed in matching purple livery. There are several people milling about, still adjusting overflowing skirts and adorning bare shoulders with gauzy shawls. The foyer, grand in nature with a domed three-story ceiling braced with curved beams, runs all the way back to a double-door entrance to a ballroom. Most people are headed in that general direction.

I scan the foyer as we walk.

Oil paintings hang on the walls, framed in gilded frames. Women I don't recognize in clothing dating back to the 16th and 17th centuries. Men with straight faces and severe mouths in clothing representing every era. There are marble pedestals installed between each painting, with some holding up marble busts, while others display ancient pottery.

The history here is tantalizing.

We finally make it to the ballroom where another staff member welcomes us to Maddred Manor. His gaze catches on Vane, mostly on the scarred eye. But really, all of him is imposing.

Does the man know that Vane's family built this house?

"Thank you for the kind welcome," Winnie says.

The man stumbles over his response before finally saying, "You're thanks."

It's not nice to laugh at someone clearly flustered by power and presence, but I've been where he's been before and every time I think of my flubs, it makes me snicker.

So I clamp my teeth together, trying to hold back the secondhand amusement.

Inside the ballroom, we find the party well underway.

Darkland loves its dark and cozy parties (though sometimes cozy is just code for "discreet debauchery") and this one is no different. The overhead lighting has been turned off, while string lights have been strung back and forth over the ballroom's length. The sconces have been lit, but they don't flicker and dance like the gas lighting of the Umbrage. This kind is something more modern, more consistent in illumination.

Outside, the heat of the day has faded replaced by a soft ocean breeze, but inside Maddred Manor, the chill of night has seeped in early. It's frigid. But oddly, all of the numerous fireplaces are dark and cold.

No fire.

No fire anywhere.

Fire is considered the coziest of all.

Alarm bells start ringing in my head.

There's a puzzle piece I know fits into place here, but it's blurry, a little out of my reach.

We walk the perimeter of the room until we spot Malachi over by the drinks.

Vane heads straight there. "Where is she?"

"Whoa. Slow down." Malachi offers Vane a drink.

Vane takes it and slings it back. Is he on edge? Either he's on edge or impatient because he says, "I don't have all night," right after slamming the glass down on the nearest table.

I stand to the side, examining Malachi.

He has his own drink in his right hand. He sips casually from it.

More alarm bells.

He looks the same. Sounds the same. But there is a sensation running up my arms, lifting the hair at the nape of my neck and when I step one step to the left, something about his face shifts, like he isn't quite there.

But when I look again, the aberration is gone. I have to refrain from reaching out to him just to see if he's real. If he's not, it'll be obvious. If he is, then I'm crazy.

I wrack my brain for more clues.

There is something about the lack of fire that's bothering me.

"I'll take you to her," Malachi finally says. "But only you."

"Fine," Vane answers, because that was always the plan, but now that Malachi has demanded it, I'm not so sure we should stick with it.

"Vane," I start, but he cuts me off.

"Don't leave each other's side. I'll only be a moment."

Malachi leads him across the ballroom and they quickly disappear from sight.

CHAPTER TWENTY-THREE
HOOK

I watch the Crocodile from across the cab as we make our way to his childhood home.

Is he on the verge of breaking? Is he a second away from shifting and devouring me whole?

It's not unlike watching an actual crocodile stalking from beneath the surface of dark, murky waters. It's impossible to know what might trigger him, what small, infinitesimal sign might proceed the destruction of his hunger.

Wendy sits beside him, her arm linked with his. Firecracker is curled up in the small space between them. Roc insisted the cat join us and I didn't have the heart to argue with him.

His head is lulled back against the wall of the carriage, his eyes closed. I can't tell if he's sleeping, focusing, or dreaming.

I don't like seeing him unwell. He's immortal. He shouldn't be sick.

And what if he turns, and it's the last time?

What if we lose him?

Pocket watch in hand, I watch the minutes tick by. It takes us exactly twenty-three to reach the house.

Wendy fidgets as we wind our way up the drive.

Is he going to be all right? she mouths to me.

"Yes," Roc answers, his eyes still closed.

Wendy widens her gaze at me and I give her a quick shake of my head.

Even taken hostage by a dark witch, it is impossible to hide anything from him. Will we ever grow accustomed to his supernatural abilities? Wendy and I may share the witch's original power, but we are not as powerful as the Crocodile. More beast than man. More myth than mortal flesh.

At the manor's entrance, Roc stumbles out ahead of us. Firecracker darts forward, disappearing into the shadows. This was why I didn't want to bring him. I'm not chasing a stray cat!

I give Wendy my hand and help her out of the cab, then pay the man with a crumpled bill.

"Roc," I call. "Crocodile!"

He's already up the stairs and entering the house.

"He might tell us he is all right," Wendy says, taking up her skirt so she can race up the stairs beside me, "but he's not acting all right."

"I don't know if this was such a good idea." We reach the third set of steps. Roc is already out of sight. "He's unstable. Unpredictable."

"He needs Vane's blood."

"And if we can't find Vane?"

Up the last flight, we hurry into the house, past the staff.

We stumble into a grand foyer dotted with partygoers.

Down the hall, I spot Roc disappearing to the left, down a hall just before the ballroom.

I race after him, Wendy doing her best to trail after me.

The hall is dark, giving the attendees the indication that it's supposed to be off limits. Roc slams into a closed door, then rattles the handle finding it locked. He reels back, then rams his shoulder into it, gaining entrance with a split of wood.

"Lainey!" he shouts.

"Bloody hell."

"That can't be good." Wendy charges ahead.

Roc is in a library with a grand piano tucked in the corner beneath a floor-to-ceiling bookshelf. Leather-bound books fill the shelves.

"Lainey," he says, softer now, a little wobbly.

"Roc." I approach him slowly. He's at the piano, hand trailing along the closed lid. "Can you hear me?"

He stops, his chin coming to his shoulder as he turns toward me. "Where's Lainey?"

I swallow. I'm in over my head. Maybe we never should have separated. Only Vane knows how to deal with whatever this is. Only he knows how to stabilize his brother and prevent the worst from happening.

I've sailed choppy waters and fought hordes of other pirates, but this, the infamous Crocodile, wounded and broken, this is something I do not know how to handle.

"She isn't here," I tell him, keeping my steps slow. "I'm not sure when she'll be back."

He curses beneath his breath and bows his head. Moonlight filters in through the closed, gauzy drapes. It paints his dark hair in strokes of silver. "Captain," he says now, his voice husky.

"Yes. I'm here."

I come around him. His eyes are squeezed shut.

"I'm having trouble fighting her," he admits.

The witch.

"She has me chasing ghosts."

Wendy comes up behind him and slips her arms around his waist, embracing him from behind. "We're here. We'll be your anchors."

He slides his hand over Wendy's, threading their fingers together.

"I can hear my father's voice in this room. Do you know his favorite saying?"

We don't, so we say nothing.

"*'You are the bane of my existence.*" He bows his head again. "From the moment I was born, he twisted my name into an insult."

"Your name?" I ask, desperate to possess it but terrified of the implications. He's hidden his name for a reason. Because I suspect he doesn't like it. Possessing it would mean holding a part of him he'd rather not share. The intimacy of that fact is one that cannot be denied.

His eyes pop open and it takes him a beat to focus on me. "Bane," he answers. "Our mother fancied herself a poet. She loved Edgar Allan Poe. Bane. Vane. And Lane. The rhyming three." He laughs, but it's thick with emotion. "Can you take me to my room?"

"Of course," I say, trying not to react to the fact that he's shared his true name. The thing he's protected above all else. "Which way?"

"There's a back staircase just beyond this hallway."

"Come." I gesture for him to put his arm around me, and Wendy positions herself on the other side. His weight is heavy on us both, but we move forward, desperate for something that will help him.

Out of the library, the noise of the party filters down the hall.

"Left," Roc says and we move, the din fading as we slip further into the house.

We find the stairwell tucked between a pantry and a storeroom. It's narrow, unadorned, meant for servants. We make our way up the first flight, unsteady, bumping into one another. We readjust on the first landing, then make our way up the second.

"Here," Roc says. "To the right."

The scones have been lit on the second floor, but only every other, making the hall dim, just enough to see our steps.

It's quieter up here, colder even. Roc directs us down the hall, then down another, until we're in the back of the house and approaching a set of closed double doors.

Roc pulls away from us and pushes the doors in.

I'm greeted with the overwhelming smell of him.

Spice and musk and bourbon.

I didn't realize it until this moment just how much the presence of him, the sight and smells and touch of him, has embedded itself into my skin.

I'm covered in goosebumps, and it's not the cold.

He goes to the barren fireplace. It's a monstrous thing, as tall as he is and twice as wide, the mantle a carved piece of marble depicting a raven's head, the beak wide open, cawing at those who stand before it.

Roc moves around the fireplace like he knows what he's doing, making a pile of kindling on the grate. He strikes a long match, the end wicking to life. The kindling catches easily, and then he's stacking logs around it, nurturing the flame until the fire burns to life.

Heat immediately fills the room.

"I'm sorry," he says, his back still to us.

"For what?" Wendy asks.

"I shouldn't have brought you both here. This is my mess to clean up."

I've never heard him sound so...*defeated*.

I want to do something. I want to reassure him. I want to fix him.

But all of this is so new, still so raw. I don't know how to care for anyone, most of all myself.

Poor form, Captain.

I am failing him.

I only know how to bark orders, how to organize things into precise lines, how to test the wind and choose a direction.

Wendy and I lock eyes. Any words exchanged between us would immediately be decoded by the Crocodile.

And yet, I think there is understanding. I see my doubt and apprehension mirrored on her face. It strikes me for the first time that she and I may be experiencing some of the same things: the constant shock of being here with Roc, the fear of being denied by him, and the all-consuming need for him.

We are the kindling hungry for his flame. There is only one way to burn, and that's beneath his attention.

I see the moment Wendy makes her decision. Her jaw sets, her nostrils flare.

I may be a pirate captain, but Wendy was always the one who knew how to take charge.

The fact that she went from prisoner to queen should surprise no one, though I think most days it still surprises her.

Another likeness between her and I: we are always doubting our agency, our own power.

She goes to him at the fireplace mantle.

In the flickering light, her dress glitters and shines like twilight.

"I'm glad we're here," she tells him. "Because all three of us...we are all stained by trauma and regrets. We understand one another in a way no one else can."

Roc huffs out a laugh. "You tell a beast that you understand it?"

"Even a monster has a heart."

His arm propped up on the mantle, he looks over at her. "Yes, but does the monster know how to use it?"

"If he doesn't, he can learn."

I can practically hear his smile. "I'm curious how these lessons would go."

Without missing a beat, Wendy slips in beneath his arm, runs her fingers back through his hair, dragging his mouth down to hers.

I can tell by the tension in Roc's back that he's caught off guard. It takes him a few seconds to catch up, to fall into the rhythm of being kissed.

His arm drops from the mantle and wraps around Wendy, pulling her into him.

It's silent in the room save for the crackling of the fire, so it's impossible for me to miss the wet press of their lips, the slide of their tongues, and watching it, hearing it, has my stomach tightening, my cock hardening.

Roc turns them, then walks Wendy back, dropping them both into a nearby chair. He spreads his legs out, sinking into the seat, positioning Wendy in his lap so that she's straddling him. His hands disappear into her hair, wrapping it around his fist, taking charge even though it was Wendy who initiated it.

My mouth goes dry.

I don't know what to do with myself.

Leave them?

Just sit and watch?

This must have been how Wendy felt when she stumbled in on us in the Everland palace. Out of place. An outsider. And yet wanting to join, not knowing how.

Thankfully, Roc knows how to lead a threesome. Because while his tongue is deep in Wendy's mouth, he still manages to snap his fingers at me, coaxing me over.

I jump at the command without even thinking.

I'm chair-side in a second, gazing down at them, both of them perfect in their own way.

Roc pulls Wendy back. Her lips are swollen and red and wet.

"I want to watch you suck the Captain's cock. Will you do that for me?"

She nods eagerly.

"Get over here, Captain."

My stomach churns, the tightness sinking to my balls.

"Where...how..." I don't know what I'm doing. I position myself at the back of the chair, just over Roc's left shoulder.

"Don't ask questions," he tells me, implying that I should take orders instead. "Unzip yourself."

I fumble with the belt, the metal clattering loudly. Once it's unlatched, Roc reaches behind him, grabbing the belt by the clasp, yanking it out of the belt loops with one quick pull. The momentum forces my hips forward, knocking me into the chair. Wendy helps, her smaller hands popping open the button.

I can't hear the rasp of the zipper over the loud beating of my heart. Suddenly, I'm exposed, hitting cool air, then the warmth of her hand.

The relief is an ocean wave.

Roc fists Wendy's hair, guiding her forward.

"Take him in your mouth," he tells her and, leaning over his shoulder, teases me first with her tongue, a light trace of her lips over the head.

I hiss out and move closer, desperate for the full heat of her.

Driving her movements, Roc pushes her into me and suddenly I'm sheathed in her. All of her.

I groan out, hips pitching forward.

She sucks eagerly, maybe desperate to perform for Roc, maybe desperate to feel something other than this ever-yawning void.

I know we all feel it.

Her tongue flattens against the underside of my shaft as Roc pulls her back, licking me from base to head.

"Just like that," Roc says. "Don't stop."

With his guidance, she quickens her pace, coaxing me closer to the edge.

I'm so fucking hard, it almost hurts. I chase the feel of her, the wetness of her tongue, the heat of her mouth, the way she pops off my dick with swollen, red lips. And then she's covering me again, eyes tearing up as I hit the back of her throat, deep, deeper.

"You can take him," Roc says, his other hand coming to her jaw, fingers pressed into her, commanding every one of her movements. "When he comes, don't swallow it. Share it with me."

"Bloody hell," I huff out, careening closer and closer to the wave crest.

It may be Wendy pleasing me, but it is undeniably both of them, and there's something dirty and illicit and so fucking right about it.

Wendy finds a rhythm, inhaling deeply through her

nose, taking me so deep that my eyes practically roll back. And then I'm breaking. I can't hold back. I push my hips forward, pursuing the feel of her. She gags. I come, grunting into her. She tries to pull back, but Roc keeps her steady until I've emptied myself into her mouth.

Finally, he lets her up and she straightens, cum glistening on her lips. Hair tangled around his hand, he yanks her mouth to him, his tongue darting into her.

I stagger back.

They are lost in the kiss, the deepness of it, the glide of their tongues against one another, my cum glistening between them. Roc groans into her and she mewls, her hips grinding against him.

Fuck.

Fucking bloody fucking hell.

Poor form. Good form? I don't fucking know.

It's the most illicit thing I've ever witnessed.

When they've swallowed back my pleasure, Roc stands, lifting Wendy in his arms. He staggers forward, snaps his fingers at me again, gesturing for me to sit on the bench at the end of his bed.

I do as I'm told.

He sets Wendy on my lap, her back to my chest. Her cheeks are red, her face a sticky mess.

Roc disappears. Wendy wiggles in my lap. I'm not completely useless and instinctively, I know what she wants, what she likes. She likes to be teased, touched, caressed.

I grab a handful of her skirt and pull it up, exposing her. She's not wearing anything beneath the skirt and when my hand slides down the curve of her hip, down to her center, I find her soaking wet.

One caress has her back arching against me, her breath coming fast.

Roc returns, a glass jar in hand.

I may have come once, but I'm still half hard, instantly ready for more.

Roc quickly liberates me of my pants. Wendy spreads her legs, straddling my thighs. And Roc gets down on his knees between us. He tastes Wendy first, and she squirms on my lap, then he drags his tongue over the length of me, pleasing us both.

He works us into a frenzy until Wendy is begging for release and I'm close to coming again.

And then suddenly he's gone and I blink up at him, eyes heavy, chest light.

He unscrews the cap on the bottle and covers his hand in a clear liquid that shines in the light. Setting the bottle aside, he strokes himself, the head of his cock swelling in the cup of his hand.

Everything in my body tightens up just thinking about him invading me.

There is something indescribable, watching someone as old, as powerful as Roc chase after the pleasure of me.

Positioning his knee on the bench between our legs, he lines himself up at my hole and my gut fills with an ocean wave.

My cock hardens, sliding up Wendy's slick center and when the head of my cock hits her clit, she gasps out, pushing her hips forward to reach me again.

I don't know if there is any greater feeling than sharing in this, all three of us together. As much as I enjoy being a captain of my own ship, I don't know that I ever truly wanted to be alone.

Roc tests my opening, nudging himself inside and I hiss out.

He leans forward, capturing Wendy's breast in his mouth, her nipple between his teeth.

The way he handles us both at once is something of a talent.

He sinks in another half inch and my cock throbs for something, anything, any kind of touch.

Taking myself in the cuff of my hand, I slowly stroke upward, and because I'm nestled against Wendy, the rise of my knuckles drags over her pussy, then her clit and she moans out in response, hooking her arm up and around my neck.

Roc runs the tip of his tongue over Wendy's bright red peak, watching me as he does.

Every time his eyes land on me, I'm like a powder keg ready to burst. I can't quite contain the heat of his attention, the way it makes me feel seen but stripped bare.

He's sunk halfway inside of me now and my pace quickens, stroking myself, chasing another orgasm.

Wendy is panting in my lap, writhing against me, her fingernails digging into the back of my neck.

"Don't come without me," he chides us, a smirk on his face. He sinks in another inch, then another, until I'm full of him. And then he's fucking me, Wendy sandwiched between us.

As his hips drive forward, he props his hands on the bed on either side of me, caging us in, and sinks into me, kissing me, then Wendy and as he kisses Wendy, I pepper her neck with the heat of my mouth.

"Blood hell," I mumble, so fucking close to coming again.

"Not yet, Captain."

"I can't..." I exhale, slow my frenzied pace. Wendy moans, drags her fingernails across my face.

"I'm so close," she says.

Roc leans forward again and devours her mouth. The wetness of their tongues meeting burns heat through my abdomen, sinking lower and lower.

It almost hurts, how badly I want to come.

I lean my head back against the bed and breathe out at the ceiling, squeezing my cock as cum leaks out.

"Make our Darling come, Captain," Roc orders. "While I fill you up."

That's all I needed to hear.

I fist myself, stroking fast, hitting Wendy's clit with every pump.

Her breathing quickens, her body tensing up and then—

She lets out a loud, shrill moan, trembling on top of me.

I can't hold on any longer. I pump hard and fast and blow all over her pussy, making a complete mess of her.

Roc's rhythm grows more frenzied and he pulls back, looming over us both as he comes inside of me.

I can't see Wendy's face, but I imagine it's no different than mine—reverence, awe, pride in having him and giving him pleasure.

When the Crocodile comes, everything that makes him terrifying fades away, replaced by the unguarded pleasure of being a man.

He stays inside of me for several beats, his breathing labored, his chest glistening, his hair damp and unkempt. His tattoos, dark against his skin, slick with sweat.

Finally, he pulls out and stumbles back. He disappears into an attached room, returning with a warm, wet cloth. He cleans Wendy first, then me, and I can't help but flush.

No one has ever...*he's never...*

I must show my dismay because he grabs me by the wrist, just below my hook, and says, "Stop fidgeting and let me take care of you."

Wendy and I are both still, letting him clean us.

When he's done, Wendy climbs off my lap, stumbles around the bed, and collapses into it. She breathes at the ceiling. I tuck myself into my trousers and button up my pants.

Wendy props herself up on her elbows and looks between us. "I enjoyed that. The three of us."

"Are we..." I can't seem to say it. I want to say it. I want confirmation. And maybe, like Wendy, I want reassurance. "Are we...the three of us..."

I steal a glance at Roc.

He's still shirtless, but his pants are on, and he's threading his belt through the loops on his pants.

"Do we have to put a label to it?" he asks.

My heart drops.

He's avoiding looking at us now.

How can he give us aftercare one minute and then pretend we're just hooking up the next?

"And if I said yes?" Wendy counters.

She's braver than I am.

I might be afraid of what label he'd give us if pressed to give one.

Fuck partners? Just friends? I couldn't bear it. To come this far, only to realize I meant so little...

Roc pulls on his shirt just as his eyes burn to bright yellow-gold.

"Are you okay?" I ask him.

"I'm...*yes*. I'm fine."

"Your eyes—"

"Both of you stay here while I go find Vane. Don't leave this room."

"You shouldn't be alone." Wendy slips off the bed. "We can come with you—"

"No." He turns for the door. "Do not leave. Understood?" He looks at me, waiting for my acknowledgment.

"Very well."

He turns to Wendy next. She's standing by the bedside, arms crossed over her chest. She tells him nothing.

To me, he says, "Don't let her leave." Then he pulls open the doors and shuts them quickly behind him.

CHAPTER TWENTY-FOUR
ASHA

I know Winnie has been watching me.

We have drinks—a signature concoction for the night called Bloody Twilight. It tastes like licorice and cherry. I've barely sipped mine. Winnie's is already gone. She's assured me that the shadow makes it nearly impossible to get drunk. I'm not so lucky.

"What kind of look?" I ask.

We're tucked in a back corner partially hidden by a potted *calycanthus Aphrodite* bush, its bright red blooms perfuming the air around us.

"Like you're trying to undress Malachi with your mind."

"Meh. Not my type."

"Okay, but—wait, what is your type?"

Despite my objections, I *am* watching Malachi closely. But Winnie asked me a question, and when data is requested, I sometimes have difficulty denying it. "The twins have the kind of body I like. Solid and stocky."

Winnie smiles wide. "So solid. *So* stocky."

"I tend to like my men a little more detached, though. I don't do emotion well."

"So a Bash body, an emotional state like Pan. How do you like to be loved?"

"I would tell you if I knew."

She watches me quietly for several seconds. "I understand," she says. "More than you know."

We scan the ballroom again. The party is well underway, with the room very close to capacity. The dance floor is in the middle of a choreographed number, the rest of the room crowded around the perimeter to watch.

"We got off track," Winnie says. "That look you had on your face...what were you thinking about?"

I'm still eyeing the ballroom as I explain.

"Something isn't right here. Notice there are no fires? No candles? I know Darkland likes its darkness, but the women are all wearing shawls or shivering from the chill. The number one rule of throwing a party is to make guests comfortable. None of this is right."

I glance over at her briefly and find a familiar expression on her face: one of curiosity and respect. Of me? By all rights, she's the more powerful one here. If there were a hierarchy, I'd be at the bottom. And yet she's regarding me like an authority figure. Like I'm the one with the answers. Truthfully, I usually am. I am almost always the smartest person in the room. But even though I know it as a fact, I don't go around flaunting it. Or at least, I don't try to.

"You have a theory," Winnie states.

I narrow my eyes, examining the room again.

"There's no reason not to have a fire in any of the numerous fireplaces dotted around the manor. Having no fire is a choice. So..."

Malachi raises his glass to drink.

He's using his right hand.

In the warehouse, I noticed the outline of a dagger on his right arm, which usually means someone is left-handed.

This Malachi has been using his right hand tonight, not his left.

And then it clicks.

My mouth drops open.

Winnie squeezes my arm and then quickly pulls away. "Sorry. I shouldn't have assumed you were okay with physical touch. I got excited. You figured it out. I can tell."

A smile cracks over my face. "I think so."

"Let's hear it, smarty pants."

I frown at her. "I've never heard that phrase before."

"It's something people say where I'm from. Sort of. It's dated, I'll admit. Meant as a compliment, of course."

"Thanks? Anyway, there are several monsters in the Seven Isles that are wary of fire. They can be burned or killed by fire. But so can we, so having a fire is not the same as completely avoiding it. Only one creature avoids fire, not only because it burns, but because it *reveals*."

"How so?"

"Flame has two characteristics: its light is inconsistent, constantly moving, but it's also heat. That's why fire is a common component to purification spells."

"I wouldn't know," she admits. "I barely understand my own power, let alone anyone else's."

Malachi makes his way across the ballroom, drink still in hand. "There is one creature in the Seven Isles that would avoid fire because of what it reveals."

"And that is?"

"A shapeshifter."

"*Oh*. That's...not good."

"No. I don't think that's Malachi."

"Fuck," she breathes out and scans the crowd. "We need to find Vane."

I can tell the instant she goes inward, her eyes glassy and far away. "But of course, I'm having trouble connecting with him. It's been like that since we left Neverland. He's been shutting me out."

"Can you break through it?"

"Possibly. It would require calling the shadow back to me, but if he's in trouble, I don't want to leave him powerless."

Her gaze goes unfocused again, and then she grumbles. "I have nothing. I'm just going to follow in his footsteps and hope I catch something. You're more than welcome to stay. I don't want to drag you on a goose chase."

"I'm coming. If he's run into a trap, he's going to need both of us."

"I bet Vane never imagined a day when he'd need to be rescued by two girls. I'm never going to let him forget it. As soon as he's safe, of course."

She starts off across the ballroom toward the arched doorway where Malachi just disappeared.

CHAPTER TWENTY-FIVE

WENDY

"James," I say.

He sits on the bench at the end of the bed and puts his face in his hands.

I go to him, threading my arm through his, leaning my head against his shoulder. I do feel unguarded around James. Everything about him is softer, easier. I guess if I did want to share two men, they are the perfect balance. One hard, one soft. One gentle, one dangerous.

I do want them both. More than I realized. If forced to pick between the two, I would refuse. I'd heave myself into the ocean. To choose between them would be like picking between the sun or the moon.

"I know he makes it difficult to love him," I say.

James's shoulders shake with a half-hearted laugh. He pulls back and glances over at me. "I suppose if he were easy to love, it wouldn't be as much fun. Everyone would do it."

"Well, I suspect everyone *does* do it, we're just the lucky two to be delusional enough to try it for real."

He nods. "Delusional or addicted to torture."

We sit like that, arms linked, for several minutes, contemplating the predicament.

"He's afraid," I say finally, maybe guessing, maybe intuiting. Roc is hard to read, even though he pretends he's not. "I'm afraid too. I've been pushing him."

James props his hook on his thigh. "I don't know what he has to be afraid of. He's a mythological monster that eats people. It's you and I who should be afraid."

I thread my fingers with his. "It's not the violence he's afraid of."

James sighs. "Yes, I know."

"The question is, how do we pull him out? How do we help him?"

"We can only be there for him when he needs us. Show him we aren't going anywhere and then—"

The door handle rattles. My heart thumps in my chest. Has he returned already? I hope he's in a better place. Maybe we can talk through all of the things he's worried—

The door pushes open.

A shadowed figure fills up the doorway.

I know right away it's not Roc. Too short. Not stocky enough.

But then he steps into the light and...

"Crocodile?" James says, his voice catching.

He steps in, looks around, and spots his abandoned blade sitting on a nearby dresser. He grabs it and slips the sheath into his back pocket. Then, "Come with me."

"Where?"

He turns and starts back down the hall.

James frowns at me. "That was weird."

"Do we go?"

"Maybe he didn't find Vane. Maybe he's trapped in another one of those hallucinations. We shouldn't leave him on his own." James pushes off the bench and jogs after Roc and I quickly follow, knowing he's right.

CHAPTER TWENTY-SIX

ROC

He stumbles through the halls of Maddred Manor, searching for his brother.

Instead, he finds his sister.

"Lainey." Her name is a prayer. His teeth clamp together, trying to stave off the burning in his eyes. How long has it been since he saw her last? Months? Years? Centuries? He can't remember. It seems like a long time. Long enough to forget about the freckles peppering her nose. The way her eyes glinted in the light.

She laughs, then turns from him and runs. He follows her through the maze of dark halls. She's always just out of reach, her hair whipping around the next corner.

Then he's back at his bedroom.

Lainey is nowhere in sight.

His heart thumps in his ears.

Everyone you've ever loved has left you, the witch says.

No, he thinks. *Wendy is here. The Captain.*

They've run off with one another just like before.

And when you catch them again, will you take the captain's other hand?

No, he thinks again, a growl, a plea.

He pushes open the door and finds his room...

Empty.

The panic sets in.

The room spins.

No.

Did they leave him? Did they decide he was too much? Too much of everything. Trouble. Danger. Violence. Baggage.

They decided they were better off without him and his monstrous ways.

They wanted to know if he could care, if he could love, and he couldn't get the words to escape the claw of his teeth.

Monsters can't love.

Monsters have no hearts.

They've left you.

He turns from the room, stumbles.

The witch is in front of him and then behind.

She's everywhere at once, closing in.

Go here, she says.

Go there, she says.

He finds himself in the back of the house, bursting into the conservatory.

It's been years and years since anything grew there, but the air still smells faintly of citrus fruit.

He blinks into the dim moonlight pouring through the glass walls.

There are silhouettes there, several of them, many of them. Ghosts of his past.

"The guest of honor has finally arrived," a voice calls from the shadows.

A figure steps around him, a blade flashing in the moonlight.

That's his blade.

There's no time to wonder when and where he lost it. Only that he did.

And the blade comes forward, sinking into his gut.

CHAPTER TWENTY-SEVEN

VANE

This is a fucking shit show.

All of it.

The only bright side is that Win isn't here and the shadow is doing a fine fucking job of blocking her out.

It and I are on the same page about protecting her. At least we have that in common.

The question running through my head right now, plaguing me like a fucking gnat, is how the fuck did the Myth Makers find out what we are? Because only two things can stop me and Roc: mercury and a blade. A very *particular* blade. And no one on this side of the glass is supposed to know our secrets.

It's mercury currently humming through my veins. An amateur mistake, taking a drink from someone without second guessing its provenance.

Malachi, that fucker. Dead by sunrise. A promise.

Or maybe I'll drag him back to Neverland once I'm finished here and we'll use him for target practice.

I forgot what it was to be weak. Mercury makes me feel mortal. Sluggish and shaky and hot.

Right now, I can barely stay upright, let alone fight. The shadow prods at me like a dog, urging me to get up.

I can't.

In the old days, ingesting mercury would have put me out for hours. Now, I'm not so sure. The shadow will likely burn through it, but not fast enough.

There's the Myth Maker standing in front of me surrounded by more of her lackeys. There's Roc across the room, a mirror image of me: he's on his knees, swaying.

They used the mercury on me, the blade on him.

He broke the promise, as I suspected he would.

You're not supposed to be here, I think, narrowing my eyes at him.

But he's too far gone to the pain to read me.

Blood is running down his front, pooling on the stone floor and filling in its cracks.

"You Maddred brothers, so predictable," the Myth says, circling behind me. "Your egos, the size of the moon." She clucks her tongue.

I snort. "And Myths are any better? I'm not the one trying to overthrow the Seven Isles. Trying to steal what is not mine."

"Oh?" She raises a brow. "Was it not the Maddred family who tore through Wonderland? Destroyed the Heart Court?" She ducks down in front of me. "Yes, I know what you are. *Jabberwocky*."

I haven't heard that word in eons.

The longer I was on this side of the glass, the more I believed I was born to the Seven Isles.

But I wasn't.

Roc and I were born in Wonderland, our family driven out by the war between the Suits.

It was so long ago, that it became a myth in my own head. No longer my story.

I barely think about it now. Jabberwocky. We are mentioned in some of the stories, some of Wonderland's world leaking over into the Seven Isles. But no one this side of the glass would know how to identify one. So we've stayed hidden in plain sight. Hidden behind titles, wealth, and secret societies.

Apparently, we no longer have that anonymity.

"Let's see," the Myth goes on. "Ruined Wonderland. Then settled in Darkland. Was it also not you who stole the Darkland Shadow and then destroyed the *Darkland* court?"

Across the room, Roc tilts to the left. How much time does he have before he's unconscious? I might need him if we're to get out of this.

"Where is it?" the Myth asks.

"Where is what?"

"The Darkland Shadow?"

Roc and I lock eyes.

I gave it to him when he was last on Neverland. I don't know what he did with it. He clearly didn't claim it, or he wouldn't be in the predicament he's currently in. I could never shift when I had the shadow, whether I wanted to or not.

"Trust me," I say, trying to distract, "you don't want to fuck with the shadow. It nearly killed me. It'll tear you in two."

"I don't want it for myself."

My vision is slowly returning and the witch is coming into focus. She's tall, curvy, with curly black hair and lips painted a bright shade of pink.

My hesitation has her rolling her eyes. "It's not that complicated. Roc gives in to my sister. Then he—they—

claim the shadow and their rightful place on the Darkland throne."

We all suspected as much, but now that the plan is out in the open, I can do something about it. Hopefully. Maybe. So long as Win stays away and Roc doesn't die on me.

"You can't have it," Roc says, slurring his words.

The Myth laughs. "I figured you'd say that." She waves her hand at the man guarding the door. He jumps to, pulling the door open. Several more lackeys come in, dragging Wendy and Hook.

"Now, Crocodile." The Myth gestures for her guards to bring her new prisoners into the center of the room. Wendy fights them. Hook seems put out but compliant. They're forced to their knees. Knives are put to their throats.

And we're predictable?

She goes to my brother and yanks the blade from his gut.

He groans, tilts forward, blood gushing from the wound.

She's by my side in an instant, the tip of the blade—*our blade*—pressed just beneath my jawline.

"Three weaknesses. All of them in this room. How many need to die before you become amenable?"

Roc isn't looking at me now. He's trained on Wendy and Hook. All of the blood has drained from his face. All of it pooled on the floor beneath him.

"You didn't leave," he says.

"What?" James asks.

"I thought...I thought you both..." He takes in a shuddering breath.

"They did try to leave you," the Myth says above me. "Vane, too. They don't love you."

Myth Makers have a power that isn't as easy to spot.

You can't taste it. You can't see it. You can't feel it on the back of your neck.

But it weasels into your ears, into your head, and burrows in like a virus, blooming into something more.

Her words aren't directed at me, but even so, I start to believe them. Just for a second.

"Don't listen to her," I say.

The blade bites into my skin, drawing blood.

"We would never leave," Wendy says.

"She's lying," the Myth counters. "She's just trying to distract you so she can run away with James Hook, just like she did before. They will always choose each other."

Roc's brow sinks and for the first time in a long time, I see despair on his face.

"Roc," I call. The blade sinks deeper. If she keeps going, I won't have a windpipe.

With the mercury still burning through my veins, I'm at a massive disadvantage.

And then I see it—a shadow, low to the ground, darting into the room.

Is that...is that a fucking cat?

And just beyond it, through the crack in the open doorway, I see two small frames.

Win and Asha.

CHAPTER TWENTY-EIGHT

ROC

They left you, the voice in his head says.

Why fight it any longer?

Give in.

Let me take on your responsibilities.

Let me do the hard work.

No, he thinks. *They didn't leave.*

He can feel his edges fraying, his body shifting. Where once this was a power he wielded against his enemies, now it's a power he seems to have forfeited.

The witch vibrates with excitement.

Let me devour them whole.

He's trying to collect himself, but it's like gathering sand through open fingers.

Devour them or kill them, either way, the outcome is the same.

He sees the Myth Maker nod, and the guard at Wendy's side readjusts his grip on his blade.

He's going to kill her.

He can't have them, but he must save them.

"Wait," he calls.

The truth doesn't matter, he realizes. They're better off without him. He's a monster, after all, and monsters don't get happy endings.

He can save them. Right now. Right here.

"I give in," he says.

He can't see the witch trapped inside of him, but he can feel her smile.

Finally.

CHAPTER TWENTY-NINE

WENDY

Firecracker is a blurred ball of fur tearing through the conservatory. Then he launches himself at the Myth, claws out.

The Myth shrieks as Firecracker latches on her face, scraping at flesh, hissing as he does.

"Get. Off. Of. Me!" The Myth yanks the cat from her face and tosses Firecracker aside.

He lands on his feet, thank god, and disappears behind a dead potted plant.

The Myth huffs out, a dozen scratches welling on her face.

Just in time for a blade to sail through the air and thunk into her eye.

Asha bounds into the room.

Relief floods through me as fighting breaks out.

But Roc...

He's hunched forward on all fours. He's shifting. Or caught somewhere between man and monster.

He's shaking like he's chilled to the bone.

The man at my side whips his arm back, slicing open my throat.

Blood wets my skin.

I grip at it instantly, terrified of the depth, the damage.

I cry out, blood rushing through my fingers.

And then it's done. The pain gone.

They either don't know, or forgot that I have Myth Maker power, that I can heal.

Asha is by my side in an instant. She leaps on the guard, a blade in each hand. She drives them down into his shoulders. He howls so loudly it makes my ears ring.

He slams back against the stone, Asha on top of him, and then she's driving the blades again into his heart.

"Your Majesty," she says, a little breathless, a little jovial, like we've just met up for a walk in the park.

"You have perfect timing," I tell her.

She smiles, then, "Duck."

I hit the ground. She throws a dagger. Another guard down. Then she's running, retrieving blades, killing again.

Beside me, James has his hook buried to the hilt inside the gut of the woman who was guarding him.

Across the room, Roc stands up.

He's stop shifting, the shape of him solid and real, except his eyes are different. Violet, not green.

He stalks toward us.

"James," I say.

"I see it," he says.

We stand shoulder to shoulder, braced.

"I think you have something that belongs to me," Roc says, but his voice is hollow and raspy, not his own. He comes to a stop in front of James, a knife in his hand. "I would like it back."

"Roc," I say. "Fight this. *Fight her.*"

He slowly turns his attention to me.

My heart thumps wildly in my ears. I've always known he's dangerous, that he could turn on me at any moment, but I don't think I've ever felt so breakable as I do right now. Because all of him is gone, any part of him that might have loved me is buried beneath the witch. Where Roc showed me care and love, the witch will show me none.

"He gave in," the witch says through his lips. "He doesn't want all of the messiness that comes with whatever this is. You begged and pleaded with him to declare his love and did he?"

I swallow. "I know he loves us."

"Does he?"

"Yes!"

"If he did, wouldn't he have fought harder?"

Tears blur my vision.

"Come back to us," I plead. "Please."

James steps between us, using his body as a shield.

"There is nothing you can say to change his mind," the witch says through Roc's mouth.

I grit my teeth, hold my breath.

"You're wrong," James argues. "Do you remember, Crocodile? *'Just six words.'*"

Roc inhales.

"But I don't need six. I just need three."

I don't know what this is, but it seems to shake Roc awake. A flicker of emotion. A glint of consciousness.

I know this is something I wasn't a part of. I know it came before me. But I don't care. I will no longer hide, I will no longer shrink away from the discomfort of loving some-one. And I sure as hell won't give in to jealousy.

I stand beside James and squeeze his hand, urging him on.

James takes a breath. "We," he says. "Love. *You.*"

Roc blinks and a single tear escapes the corner of his eye.

"I love you too," he says, and then, "*Run.*"

CHAPTER THIRTY

HOOK

THE CROCODILE'S TRANSFORMATION IS AS SWIFT AS A STORM cloud rolling in.

He brings the darkness, the wreckage, the chaos.

Asha runs toward us, Vane and Winnie just behind her.

The Myth Maker is on her feet, a dagger stuck in her eye, half her face covered in blood. Of course she wouldn't be dead. Myths are hard to kill.

But the Crocodile is on her in an instant, devouring her whole.

I grab Wendy by the wrist and yank her from the room. "We need that hat. Now. *Malachi*—"

"He was a shapeshifter," Asha says. "I don't think that was the same Malachi we met."

"He has to be somewhere in the manor, don't you think?" Winnie says.

Screaming tears through the air behind us.

We're all running down the hallway, directionless.

"If you were holding someone hostage in your manor," Asha asks Vane, "where would you hide him?"

More screams. Glass breaks.

"The wine cellar," Vane decides.

"How do we get there?"

"This way."

We change directions, go down a flight of stairs to the first floor. In the distance, the party is still in full swing, everyone in attendance oblivious to the chaos going on just out of their sight.

Through another hall, down another flight of stairs, we come to a damp stone floor, chilly air.

There's a single sconce flickering from the wall to the left.

Vane disappears into the cellar's depths, but his voice echoes back to us. "There are seven holding rooms down here," he explains, checking one, then a second. "The third has a hidden room…" He disappears inside. "There you are, you fucker."

We gather into the small room surrounded by honeycomb shelves full of bottled wine. One of the shelves has been pushed in revealing a hidden alcove where more kegs are held. Malachi is inside, gagged and tied up.

Vane undoes the gag. "Tell me you have the hat."

"Thanks. Nice to see you, too. I've only been stuck down here in the dark for many fucking hours," Malachi says.

Vane crouches beside him. "Tell me you have the hat, or I'm feeding you directly to my brother. Bones and all."

Malachi licks his lips. "Fine. Yes. I have the hat. Is the Myth gone?"

"The Crocodile just ate her," I say. "That's two Myths he's devoured. We need that hat right fucking now."

"I left it in the library. In the piano."

We were just in there earlier. We were so fucking close to it. It was within our reach.

Asha stays behind to untie Malachi while Vane, Winnie, Wendy, and I return to the library.

The piano hood is opened, the hat revealed.

I'm not sure what I expected, but a crushed velvet top hat was not it.

Vane retrieves it with a careful grip.

"It's really a hat?" Winnie says.

"I said it was a hat," Vane answers.

"Yeah, but I was sorta expecting that to be some kind of metaphor."

"It's a hat," he says and makes his way back upstairs.

"But like...a magical hat?" Winnie asks.

"Something like that."

We approach the open doors to the conservatory with apprehension, with urgency beating at our backs.

It's silent inside.

All of the bodies are gone, all of the Myth Maker's guards.

There is only the Crocodile, propped up against the outer wall, blood covering his face, his neck, crusted beneath his fingernails. Firecracker is batting at a torn piece of fabric hanging from Roc's shirt.

When we enter, he looks up slowly, sees the hat, and laughs. "Fucking finally."

He sets the cat aside, then struggles to all fours and vomits black ichor.

When he's done heaving, he collapses to his side. "Hurry."

"Get up." Vane is by his side. I quickly take the other and together we hoist Roc to his knees. To me, Vane says, "When I put the hat on him, you stand back. Far back."

What kind of hat is this anyway?

"You ready?" Vane asks his brother.

Roc trembles, then nods.

Vane holds the hat over Roc's head like he's about to place a crown. It's deliberate, slow, calculated.

I can't feel my legs, but I'm determined to run the second it's on Roc's head.

Time seems to slow.

My ears ring.

When the hat is finally placed, the air snaps.

I let Roc go and race across the room, pulling Wendy behind me.

Vane takes Winnie, then Asha.

Light flickers over the room. Bright red, then silver, then red again. The flashing intensifies, snapping like lightning.

Roc's hands curl into fists. The sound he makes is more monstrous than any he's ever uttered. A primordial roar.

The ground vibrates beneath us. I pull Wendy into my side, tight against my hip.

In the flickering light, veins pop across Roc's forehead as he grits his teeth.

And then—

Silence.

The sudden absence of the flashing light has me momentarily blind.

When my vision adjusts, I spot Roc across the room face down on the stone. The hat has come off and rolled on its side.

Wendy and I race to him, our footsteps echoing across the conservatory.

"Thank god, he's breathing." Wendy drops to her knees. "Roc?"

"I need a drink," he mutters.

Wendy groans, but there's a smile of relief pulling at the corners of her mouth.

"Is the witch gone?" I ask him.

Slowly, he climbs to all fours, then sits back on his ass. "Yeah. She's gone. Along with her sister."

Asha, Winnie, and Vane come up behind us.

"You dumb shit," Vane says.

Roc gets up on his feet. He stares down at Vane. "I love you too," he says and then wraps Vane in a hug.

Vane is stiff for all of two seconds, and then he hugs his brother back.

"Thank you," Roc says.

"Stop devouring every random inconvenience. We only have one hat. If something happens to that one, I'm not going through the glass for another."

"Don't worry. I'll behave." Then Roc plants a kiss on Vane's forehead.

Vane curses beneath his breath.

"*Through the glass?*" Wendy mouths to me.

I shrug. I've never heard either of them reference glass.

When Roc breaks away from Vane, he comes over to me and Wendy. He's still covered in blood, his clothing in tatters. But he pulls us in. "I love you too," he says. "I guess I need four words."

We laugh.

"I need to hear that story," Wendy says.

"I'll do one better," Roc tells her. "I'll show you."

Bloody hell. Thank god it's dark in the conservatory because I'm fucking blushing.

"Now come on. I was serious about that drink." He makes his way for the door. "And I suppose we need to discuss whether or not I'm making a claim on my title."

"You can't seriously be considering becoming king—" Vane is cut off by a sharp look from Winnie. A silent conversation passes between them.

"You're right," Vane finally says. "I need a fucking drink."

CHAPTER THIRTY-ONE

ROC

I feel like I've dropped a century. All of the aches and pains are gone. All of the wisdom of age, none of the hubris of youth. I feel like I could conquer the world.

But I don't want to get ahead of myself.

I go to the smoking room just past the ballroom. When I was a child, my father and his friends would retire here after dinner parties to smoke and drink and do fuck all.

There's a full bar and countless bottles of every liquor you can imagine.

The man behind the counter gives me an odd look when I join him. But then he recognizes me, gives me a shaky, awkward bow, then stutters over his words. "Is t-t-there any— anything I can get you, sir?"

"Yeah," I say, "you can get the fuck out of my way."

He's gone in an instant leaving me to the bar.

I pour myself a bourbon twice the normal size and swig it back.

The others gather around the bar watching me intently, like they aren't sure if I'm myself again or if I'll snap and start eating fingers and toes.

"Stop looking at me," I warn them, then line up several glasses on the bartop and fill each with a shot of bourbon. "We won."

Vane slides onto a stool and takes his drink in hand. "We won the battle, but did we win the war?"

I shrug and refill my glass. "The Myth Makers are down one Myth, and down a witch. And now they have lost Darkland."

Wendy and the Captain take a seat. "And the plan now?" the Captain asks.

I sling back the second drink. The alcohol soothes some of the buzzing energy filling my veins. The hat has that effect. It's like the world's best juice cleanse.

"For most of my life," I say, "I've been running from who I am. Maybe it's time I stop."

Wendy takes her drink and tips it back, wincing at the burn. "If you're staying, I'm staying."

I turn to the Captain. "And you?"

His nostrils flare. "Where you go, I follow."

"Just three words?" I repeat.

He runs his tongue along the inside of his bottom lip. He's doing that on purpose, dragging my gaze to his fucking mouth. "I'll use six if you're giving them," he says.

I wink at him. "Six will do."

CHAPTER THIRTY-TWO
VANE

Before Winnie and I leave Darkland, we have a few things to wrap up. I need to know that the hat is stored in a safe place and that Roc is stabilized, and isn't off running his fucking mouth, getting himself into more trouble.

We've moved into Maddred Manor.

Right now, he's sitting across from me in the room that used to be our father's office, and is now his.

The desk is different. The cloth and leather-bound books on the shelves are different. Even the handwoven carpet and the bar cart along the wall. All of it was chosen by Roc, and yet everything is in the same place it was when our father was the head of the house. It's startling how everything can change, and yet the imprint of the old remains.

"Have you decided?" I ask him.

Late morning sun pours in through the double garden doors behind him. The glass has been freshly cleaned and the light hits all of the imperfections, the bubbles and the undulating waves of unevenness. The others are still in the breakfast room, gorging themselves on the food cooked and baked by Roc's new kitchen staff. Win saw the croissants and practically melted into the floor. That girl has a weakness for baked goods. Bash has corrupted her.

Roc leans back in his chair and props his boots on the edge of the desk. He's different this morning. And not just because he's well-rested and no longer burdened by the witch.

He finally claimed the Darkland Dark Shadow.

I helped him, convinced the shadow would fight him like it fought me, that I would spend the rest of the night patching him up like he had when the shadow tried to claw its way out of me.

But Roc made it look easy. Just as he makes everything. He and the shadow were united from the onset. There was no infighting, no carnage or chaos. Just a pop of air, a swirl of darkness.

"How does it feel?" I asked him.

He had leaned back in the nearest chair and stared off into space for several long seconds. "I feel...calm, for once."

I nodded. I knew exactly what he meant.

The shadows help keep our monsters at bay. No more bowing to the god of time. No more drinking blood to stave off the turn. The shadows come with their own price, but it's much easier to pay.

The chair creaks now when Roc shifts, rolling his head along the quilted leather back so he can look over at me. "Have I made my decision?" he repeats. "Yes."

I sit forward, elbows on my knees.

"I'm going to make a claim on my title and my right to the Darkland throne."

I crack a knuckle, letting the information sink in.

I'm caught off guard by it. I didn't think—

"I can tell you're surprised."

"You hate obligations."

"I *used* to hate obligations."

"And now you don't?"

"Now I have to become something else." His gaze goes distant, in the direction of the breakfast room. He's thinking about Wendy and Hook. Two more things I'm surprised by. I knew he had an interest in Wendy all those years ago, but I thought she was a pawn. An unwitting plaything caught in a game. And Hook? He hated the captain at one time.

I was wrong.

I suppose I was wrong about a great many things, mostly both Darling women.

"Darkland King, huh?" I say.

"There aren't many people left to oppose me. And even if there were, I doubt they'd have the balls."

"Juliette?" I ask.

"Nah. She won't be a problem. She loves me, for one, and two, she had wanted to study astronomy at the Dark University. She was told she couldn't. This will give her the perfect excuse."

"Is this really what you want?"

He thinks again, his hands clasped over his stomach. "I'm tired of running, Vane."

He rarely says my name. It's too close to his, the one he was born with, the one he detests.

Hearing him say it, I realize...he has changed. He has become something more.

"Neverland will support you and your claim," I say. "You have my word."

He laughs. "You think Peter Pan will agree with you?"

"Leave Pan to me."

"Gladly." He stands up and comes over to me, waggling his fingers. I grunt and stand so he can wrap me in an aggressive hug. "Thank you for coming to my aid," he says.

"I couldn't have you devouring half the Seven Isles."

"At least a third of them fuckers deserve to be devoured."

From the breakfast room, Win calls my name. Roc and I break apart and I make my way to the door.

"You're welcome," I tell him, half in the hallway, hand on the doorframe. He and I have been alive a very long time. We've made new families, formed new friendships, but he and I are all that remain of our old life. I thought I had left that behind, but in this moment, I'm glad to have him back.

"The Madd Brothers reunited," he says. "Go on. Your Darling calls."

I nod and follow the pull of my own shadow, the pull of my Darling.

EPILOGUE
ROC

THE WAREHOUSE IS AS WE LEFT IT, WITH A FAINT TRACKING OF OUR footprints in the accumulated dust.

There's so much history here, some of it I'd rather stay buried.

Vane and I make our way through the aisles of stacked crates and shelves to the back of the warehouse, where half the Variant Collection is stored in an oak cabinet.

The front is unadorned save for a thick iron lock.

I have to admit, I'm impressed Malachi managed not only to locate our warehouse, break inside, but also pick the cabinet lock. Impressed, yes, but also annoyed. How did he manage it? I have half a mind to recruit him. Maybe I will, if I can talk him out of returning to Lostland to the infighting of the Myths.

Using our skeleton key, I unlock the bolt and pull the doors open.

The others are gathered behind us, peering over our shoulders.

"It really is just a hat collection?" Wendy says, the disappointment clear in her voice.

I glance back at her. "Did you expect something else when I said 'hat collection'?"

She shrugs. "In the Seven Isles, anything can be anything."

I suppose she isn't wrong.

There's an empty spot on the middle shelf for the oldest hat, *the first hat*, the one used to remove that which is devoured.

It was crafted by our uncle, as was the rest of them.

Some of the hats give the wearer power. Some affect the wearer in different ways, like the devourer hat. Some take, some give, some transform.

There are more top hats, a few fedoras, an eight-piece tweed cap, and two flat caps. All of them were stretched, shaped, and stitched by hand.

I set the devourer hat on its iron stand.

"Have you ever worn the others?" Wendy asks.

"Of course." I shut the cabinet and reinstall the lock. "But not for a very long time now. Haven't really had a need."

Winnie sidles up next to Vane, her hand curled around his bicep. "What other treasures do you have in this warehouse? What other secrets of the Maddred Brothers can we uncover here?"

"No," my baby brother says, an all-encompassing answer.

We have a great many secrets. Too many. Too many that should remain secrets.

Winnie and Wendy lock arms, giggle to one another, and disappear between two stacks of crates.

"Win," Vane says with a grumble.

"Oh don't mind me." Her voice filters up, swirling around the high warehouse ceiling. "Just having a look."

"Do not, under any circumstances, touch a hat," Vane says, chasing after her.

The Captain comes to my side. "Do you just leave magical hats lying around for any unsuspecting person to stumble on?"

"No," I tell him, but my smile contradicts me.

"You are merciless."

"And soon I will be insufferable." I swat his ass. He huffs out with indignation. "As soon as the paperwork is filed and my title reclaimed, the throne mine, I will be your king. Imagine all of the vile things I will demand of you."

He licks his lips, heat rising up his throat. "Demand what you want. I bow to no man."

"I am no man, Captain."

"Nor monsters."

I laugh. "We'll see about that."

"Christ," I hear Vane say from deep within the stacks.

"Who was she?" I hear Winnie ask.

I know immediately who she's referring to and what artifact from our past she has uncovered.

Christ is an understatement.

The Captain gives me a suspicious look. His curiosity gets the better of him and he's soon trailing after the conversation.

"She was no one," I hear my brother say, which yes, huge understatement number two.

I follow in the Captain's footsteps.

Wendy, Winnie, Vane, and Asha are gathered around a seven-foot oil painting.

It was commissioned so long ago that the varnish has cracked and turned yellow.

I'm on the left, Vane on the right. And in between us is a girl, half our size. Somehow, she takes up more space on the canvas. Her back is to Vane, but his hand is on her hip. Her body is turned toward me, but her attention is on the viewer. Those dark brown eyes. So dark, they're almost black.

She's wearing the eight-piece cap and a matching tweed vest. The hat was specially made for her.

The sheet that had been draped over the painting lies on the floor, pooled around the gilded frame.

I hate this painting, and yet I've never been able to part with it. It's a reminder of how everything can be ripped away, how trust and loyalty are always thin, and obsession can make you mad.

"Who was she?" Wendy asks me, echoing Winnie.

Darling women never relent.

"A ghost from our past," Vane says.

"Who?" Wendy persists.

"Al," I say because that's what we called her.

"Alice," Vane corrects. "Her name was Alice."

Seeing her face again puts flame to the rage. I buried thoughts of her a long time ago, along with all of the artifacts in this warehouse.

"Come on." I toss the sheet back over the painting. "She's long gone. Vane is right, she's no one to worry about now."

Either they have decided to show us mercy, or their curiosity has already burned out. They take the answer and file out toward the door.

I meet Vane's gaze.

No one to worry about? Maybe. Probably. Alice slipped through the glass a long time ago. And hopefully she stays there, with our mad uncle.

Because if she ever shows her face here again, I'll kill her myself.

Vane and I head toward the door and flick off the lights. Outside the warehouse, we click the lock into place.

As far as I'm concerned, this part of our past should stay buried for good.

VANE AND THE CROCODILE ONCE RULED THE DARKLAND UNDERWORLD...

AFTER THEIR FATHER'S FAILED COUP, VANE AND ROC WERE stripped of their titles and their assets. Immortal, powerful and monstrous, it didn't take them long to make their way back up the ladder, but it wasn't in the manors and mansions of the Darkland elite, it was in the dark underbelly known as the Umbrage.

Years later, they now rule the Umbrage and they are ruthless, destroying anyone who gets in their way. But even monsters have hearts, and when Roc and Vane find theirs broken, there's only one choice: get revenge.

Go back to where it all began in...

DARK & DARKER STILL: A VANE AND ROC ORIGIN STORY

PRE-ORDER NOW!

SCAN ME

ALSO BY NIKKI ST. CROWE

DEVOURER DUOLOGY

Devourer of Men

Devour the Dark

VICIOUS LOST BOYS SERIES

The Never King

The Dark One

Their Vicious Darling

The Fae Princes

WRATH & RAIN TRILOGY

Ruthless Demon King

Sinful Demon King

Vengeful Demon King

Wrath & Reign Omnibus

HOUSE ROMAN

A Dark Vampire Curse

MIDNIGHT HARBOR

Hot Vampire Next Door: Season One

Hot Vampire Next Door: Season Two

Hot Vampire Next Door: Season Three

Hot Vampire Next Door: Season Four

Hot Vampire Next Door: Season Five

Ink & Feathers

ABOUT THE AUTHOR

NIKKI ST. CROWE has been writing for as long as she can remember. Her first book, written in the 4th grade, was about a magical mansion full of treasure. While she still loves writing about magic, she's ditched the treasure for something better: villains, monsters, and anti-heroes, and the women who make them wild.

These days, when Nikki isn't writing or daydreaming about villains, she can either be found in the woods or at home with her husband and daughter.

THE GARDEN NEWSLETTER
https://nikkistcrowe.myflodesk.com/thegarden

FOLLOW NIKKI ON INSTAGRAM
www.instagram.com/nikkistcrowe

NIKKI'S SUBSTACK:
https://nikkistcrowe.substack.com/

VISIT NIKKI ON THE WEB AT:
www.nikkistcrowe.com

instagram.com/nikkistcrowe

amazon.com/author/nikkistcrowe

facebook.com/authornikkistcrowe

youtube.com/@crowehouse

threads.net/@nikkistcrowe

bookbub.com/profile/nikki-st-crowe

www.ingramcontent.com/pod-product-compliance
Lightning Source LLC
Chambersburg PA
CBHW031043310726
48969CB00007B/2089